PRAISE FOR THE PLAYS O

REASONS TO BE PRETTY

"Mr. LaBute is writing some of the freshest and most illuminating American dialogue to be heard anywhere these days . . . *Reasons* flows with the compelling naturalness of overheard conversation. . . . It's never easy to say what you mean, or to know what you mean to begin with. With a delicacy that belies its crude vocabulary, *Reasons to be Pretty* celebrates the everyday heroism in the struggle to find out."
—**Ben Brantley**, *The New York Times*

"[T]here is no doubt that LaBute knows how to hold an audience. . . . LaBute proves just as interesting writing about human decency as when he is writing about the darker urgings of the human heart." —**Charles Spencer**, *Telegraph*

"[F]unny, daring, thought-provoking . . ." —**Sarah Hemming**, *Financial Times*

IN A DARK DARK HOUSE

"Refreshingly reminds us . . . that [LaBute's] talents go beyond glibly vicious storytelling and extend into thoughtful analyses of a world rotten with original sin."
—**Ben Brantley**, *The New York Times*

"LaBute takes us to shadowy places we don't like to talk about, sometimes even to think about . . ."
—**Erin McClam**, *Newsday*

WRECKS

"Superb and subversive . . . A masterly attempt to shed light on the ways in which we manufacture our own darkness. It offers us the kind of illumination that Tom Stoppard has called 'what's left of God's purpose when you take away God.'"
—**John Lahr**, *The New Yorker*

"[*Wrecks* is a] tasty morsel of a play . . . The profound empathy that has always informed LaBute's work, even at its most stringent, is expressed more directly and urgently than ever here."
—**Elysa Gardner**, *USA Today*

"*Wrecks* is bound to be identified by its shock value. But it must also be cherished for the moment-by-moment pleasure of its masterly portraiture. There is not an extraneous syllable in LaBute's enormously moving love story."
—**Linda Winer**, *Newsday*

FAT PIG

"The most emotionally engaging and unsettling of Mr. LaBute's plays since *bash* . . . A serious step forward for a playwright who has always been most comfortable with judgmental distance." —**Ben Brantley**, *The New York Times*

"One of Neil LaBute's subtler efforts . . . Demonstrates a warmth and compassion for its characters missing in many of LaBute's previous works [and] balances black humor and social commentary in a . . . beautifully written, hilarious . . . dissection of how societal pressures affect relationships [that] is astute and up-to-the-minute relevant." —**Frank Scheck**, *New York Post*

THE MERCY SEAT

"Though set in the cold, gray light of morning in a downtown loft with inescapable views of the vacuum left by the twin towers, *The Mercy Seat* really occurs in one of those feverish nights of the soul in which men and women lock in vicious sexual combat, as in Strindberg's *Dance of Death* and Edward Albee's *Who's Afraid of Virginia Woolf*." —**Ben Brantley**, *The New York Times*

"[A] powerful drama . . . LaBute shows a true master's hand in gliding us amid the shoals and reefs of a mined relationship." —**Donald Lyons**, *New York Post*

THE SHAPE OF THINGS

"LaBute . . . continues to probe the fascinating dark side of individualism . . . [His] great gift is to live in and to chronicle that murky area of not-knowing, which mankind spends much of its waking life denying."

—**John Lahr**, *The New Yorker*

"LaBute is the first dramatist since David Mamet and Sam Shepard—since Edward Albee, actually—to mix sympathy and savagery, pathos and power."

—**Donald Lyons**, *New York Post*

"*Shape* . . . is LaBute's thesis on extreme feminine wiles, as well as a disquisition on how far an artist . . . can go in the name of art . . . Like a chiropractor of the soul, LaBute is looking for realignment, listening for a crack."

—**John Istel**, *Elle*

BASH

"The three stories in *bash* are correspondingly all, in different ways, about the power instinct, about the animalistic urge for control. In rendering these narratives, Mr. LaBute shows not only a merciless ear for contemporary speech but also a poet's sense of recurring, slyly graduated imagery . . . darkly engrossing."

—**Ben Brantley**, *The New York Times*

PHOTO: AARON ECKHART

NEIL LABUTE is an award-winning playwright, filmmaker, and screenwriter. His plays include: *bash*, *The Shape of Things*, *The Distance From Here*, *The Mercy Seat*, *Fat Pig* (Olivier Award nominated for Best Comedy), *Some Girl* (s), *Reasons to be Pretty* (Tony Award nominated for Best Play), *In A Forest, Dark and Deep*, and a new adaptation of *Miss Julie.* He is also the author of *Seconds of Pleasure*, a collection of short fiction, and a 2013 recipient of a Literature Award from the American Academy of Arts and Letters.

Neil LaBute's films include *In the Company of Men* (New York Critics' Circle Award for Best First Feature and the Filmmaker Trophy at the Sundance Film Festival), *Your Friends and Neighbors*, *Nurse Betty*, *Possession*, *The Shape of Things*, *Lakeview Terrace*, *Death at a Funeral,* and *Some Velvet Morning.*

ALSO BY NEIL LABUTE

FICTION

Seconds of Pleasure: Stories

SCREENPLAYS

In the Company of Men

Your Friends and Neighbors

PLAYS

bash: three plays

The Mercy Seat

The Distance From Here

The Shape of Things

Fat Pig

Autobahn

This Is How It Goes

Some Girl(s)

Wrecks and Other Plays

In a Dark Dark House

Reasons to be Pretty

Filthy Talk for Troubled Times and Other Plays

The Break of Noon

Lovely Head and Other Plays

Miss Julie: A New Adaptation

REASONS TO BE HAPPY

THE OVERLOOK PRESS
NEW YORK, NY

First published in paperback in the United States in 2013 by
The Overlook Press, Peter Mayer Publishers, Inc.

141 Wooster Street
New York, NY 10012
www.overlookpress.com
For bulk and special sales, please contact sales@overlookny.com,
or write us at the above address.

Cataloging-in-Publication Data is available from the Library of Congress

Book design and type formatting by Bernard Schleifer
Manufactured in the United States of America
ISBN 978-1-4683-0721-4
1 3 5 7 9 10 8 6 4 2

for john lahr

"just do what must be done."

—G.B. Shaw

"if you want to be happy, be."

—Leo Tolstoy

"i once had a girl, or should i say, she once had me."

—Lennon/McCartney

PREFACE

You can't go home again.

Somebody said that—certainly once or twice before Thomas Wolfe made it famous—and while it's obviously not true in the literal sense, it certainly should be a rule to live by (unless you left something at home that's really important in which case I'd suggest hurrying there, getting it without talking to anyone and then leaving again very quickly, preferably by the back door). Life goes on and so it should and we all learn the hard way that we outgrow our childhood bedrooms and our school halls and even our families themselves. It's wonderful to look back on our individual and collective pasts, sometimes with fondness and sometimes with regret, but to live in that place is the equivalent of being stuck. It's healthy to keep moving forward and trying new things. That's not to say forget about Mom and Dad and Sis and Uncle ________ (fill in the blank) but all of us, especially those who make a living by turning the page and exploring new worlds each night on the stage, need to keep moving toward the horizon and pushing ourselves to conquer the next audition, the next role or the next production. Theater doesn't allow us to rest on our laurels for long; the life of a play is short (unless you're Andrew Lloyd Webber) and suddenly the curtain comes down for a final time and we have nothing but a program and some photos to show our friends and family who didn't make it out to see the play and we're out of a job. By its very nature, there is a magical quality to a play on stage—now you see it, now you don't.

As a writer, I am someone who keeps trying to create new characters in new stories and pushing myself to surprise my audience with something that feels both new and familiar. I'm not complaining—I love my work. I'm at my best sitting in a darkened auditorium, working with actors and technicians to create an evening of theatrical entertainment. In life I can be indecisive or distant or cowardly or secretive or just plain human. I come to life in the artificial surroundings of the playhouse. I don't know why that is—I only know and believe it to be true. This isn't always the case, of course, nothing is always true, but often enough to call it a "truth." Ironically, I am getting better at living as I get closer to dying but that's enough of that. Who wants to be so damn honest at a time like this? The publication of a new play is always a time of celebration for me; the chance to leave a record of my very ephemeral life in the theater behind is a pleasure indeed.

And after all of that preamble, the truth is I'm doing the very thing I warn the reader against: going home again. As an author I have now gone back to check in on a group of characters whom I wanted to see again and find out what has happened to them in the last few years. I've often envied television writers who get the opportunity to revisit the fictional lives of their characters week after week, year after year, and so I decided to do the same but on the stage. It's certainly been done before but it's a first for me and it was a pleasure to do so. I thought for a long while about what group of characters I might want to spend some time with again—the characters in *Fat Pig* came close and I was certainly curious to see where the people in *The Shape of Things* might be a decade later—but in the end I wanted to head back to the small Midwestern town that Greg and Steph and Carly and Kent called home. It's in the middle of nowhere (or what some folks might call "anywhere, USA") and it's a place that I don't want to live but I also feel like I've spent half of my life there. It could be a college town or the kind of rural industrial landscape of my youth or one of those suburban backwaters that exists from Florida to Maine and from the tip of California to the border towns of Washington state (and virtually any spot in between). These days, to be a person struggling to get by at work and in love is to say you're an "American." People live from paycheck to paycheck, they work late and at several jobs just trying to make ends meet and everybody has a dream, whether it's getting through trade school or running their own company or falling in love or taking one more breath. Life is hard and I get to write about that—little tragedies and victories that play out in an hour and a half—and I feel lucky when anybody says to me that what they've just seen rings even partially true.

Nothing we do on stage matters as much as life—nothing I write means as much as somebody else's birth or first communion or marriage or retirement or death—but if writers and actors and audiences can band together and play out a few stories that feel honestly created and genuinely inhabited then maybe we can find some kind of solace together for a few hours, reminding ourselves that we are all in this together and that maybe, just maybe, an imagined version of life can lead us toward how and why we should go about living the real thing. I might be full of shit, but it's meant to be inspirational shit and even now it doesn't sound completely crazy to me.

So this is the next chapter in the lives of four people in whom I hope you'll recognize yourselves (or at least your friends and neighbors). I like these guys and I've tried to give them all an opportunity to be happy and to do better and to get ahead. Some of them do good things and one or two of them even feel like they've got a real chance at writing themselves a new ending to their seemingly preordained lives. I like Greg and his bumbling attempts to be a nice guy. He makes nearly as many mistakes as I do in life and so I appreciate the way he keeps picking himself up off the ground, only to fuck up yet again. Steph is one tough chick and yet her heart is huge and I love the passion with which she lives her life, always going for broke. I had no idea where Kent would take me this time around but he surprised me a lot along the way—he just might make it as a man—and Carly is the kind of person I wish I was a little bit more like: centered and caring and disarmingly honest about herself and others.

I don't know if I've got another story about these four people inside me; we get caught up in trilogies and franchise pictures in American entertainment and I only want to keep writing these plays if I actually have something worthwhile to say. I might drop in on these folks again one day but if I don't, I'm happy where they end up this time around. It was good to see them again and I thank them for reminding me that no matter how shitty life can be, it's so much better than the alternative.

And best of all, I remembered an important aspect of living by writing *Reasons to be Happy* : enjoy the journey and don't forget to look up from time to time—the scenery is beautiful and your fellow travelers are pretty fucking interesting.

Neil LaBute
March 2013

REASONS TO BE HAPPY

Reasons to be Happy had its American premiere at the Lucille Lortel Theatre (MCC) in New York City in May 2013. It was directed by Neil LaBute.

GREG	Josh Hamilton
STEPH	Jenna Fischer
CARLY	Leslie Bibb
KENT	Fred Weller

A slash (/) indicates the point of interruption between the present line and the next speaker's line.

The text that follows represents the script as it went into rehearsals for the American premiere.

The lights pop on. Bam. Just like that.

*A parking lot. Two people—*GREG *and* STEPHANIE*—standing in front of a discount store. Both with bags of food in their arms. Smack in the middle of yet another fight.*

GREG . . . no, no, no, no!/ No, uh-uh, no!

STEPH Yes!/ Don't lie, you fucker!

GREG Steph, no! (*Beat.*) We are not gonna do this again, so just stop!

STEPH So then explain it to me . . . *liar*.

GREG Look . . . this is . . . not *here*, alright? Not in the parking lot of *Costco*, I am not willing to do that . . . / I don't have to so I won't./ I'm not gonna. No.

STEPH Fuck, that's so . . . / Of course you won't./ You won't because you *can't* is why, you won't because you don't have a fucking leg to stand on, that's how come, Greg. Not because you don't have time or that you don't need to, because you do. (*Beat.*) I think you owe me an explanation so it's not for that reason so there must be some others, right? There must be a *ton* of other reasons you don't wanna face me right now . . . / Am I right about that? Hmm?

GREG No, that's not . . . / I'm totally happy to go somewhere—not today, but some time—and sit with you and discuss this. (*Beat.*) Discuss it like people do, over *coffee* or whatever, but not like two snarling dogs off in an empty lot . . . that's ridiculous and, and . . . frankly, it's just not cool . . . so no.

GREG *is about to say something else but stops. Glances around for the cavalry to arrive. Sorry. Not today.*

STEPH So, you *won't*, then? Right? You will not?

GREG No, Steph, I won't. You can't make me.

STEPH Oh *really*? I *can't*?

GREG No . . . I mean . . . *no*! Stop!! You always have that . . . God, there's always like this sort of *threatening* tone in your voice when we fight . . . I haven't been around you for however long, years now—barely, anyway—and I get that same feeling in my stomach the second you start in like this again . . . why is that?

STEPH Maybe because you feel like shit, like a guilty fucking asshole, maybe that's why. (*Beat.*) I'm just *guessing*, but maybe.

GREG That's not . . . for *what*? What for?

STEPH You tell me, Greg. You say it for once . . . instead of me always dragging it out of you with a team of fucking Clydesdales!

GREG Oh please! (*Beat.*) I've got ice cream sandwiches in here, by the way . . . / Just so you know!

STEPH Fuck that, asshole! / Just be a man once!!

GREG This is ridiculous! It's . . . *so* . . .

STEPH Yeah it is, Greg, the whole situation is ridiculous . . . the fact that you guys have never said anything to me is ridiculous! It's pretty fucking amazing, when I think about it for even two seconds at a time!

GREG What?! I just . . . I mean . . . *why*?!

STEPH Because Carly's my friend, Greg, one of my very best friends from my life, or so I thought up until about two days ago . . .

GREG You're . . . this doesn't have anything to do with that./ Seriously. It's . . .

STEPH Oh, really?/ It doesn't?

GREG No! Who says you can't be friends?!

STEPH You! You sleeping in her bed at night . . . / That puts a real fucking kink in the *arc* of our friendship!

GREG I am not *sleeping* in . . . / We're just . . .

STEPH Doesn't matter!/ Does not!

GREG Does too!/ Yes, it *does*!

STEPH No it doesn't!!

GREG AHHHHH! Yes, it does, Stephanie!! I'm not *living* with her, okay, so yes, that's a completely different thing there. Let's just be clear about that . . . we're dating.

STEPH . . . you and your fucking *words* . . .

GREG I didn't do this to hurt you! Jesus, it's not like we, we, we . . . *planned* it.

STEPH She's not taking my calls, Greg. She lets them go to voice mail and that's a first. First time in our lives since I've known her to not pick up her phone when I call and it's 'cause of you! Ok? YOU! (*Beat.*) I mean, fuck, I didn't see *this* one coming!

GREG What's it matter, Steph . . . I mean, really? Huh?! We *found* each other, long after you and Kent were ever in the picture and . . .

STEPH So what?!

GREG So . . . why is this a big deal?! You're . . . *married* now!

STEPH . . . !!

GREG I just . . . I mean, aren't you guys moving or something? That's what I heard . . .

STEPH Maybe! We're "maybe" moving . . . or getting transferred we think, but so what? That's not the issue here . . . *you're* the issue!

GREG I'm just saying!

STEPH Then say it!/ *What*?! What're you saying?!

GREG I *am*! / Why should you care who *I'm* with?! It's none of your business . . . so just . . .

STEPH I don't! I don't give a fuck, Greg, who you're with . . . as long as it's not one of my long-time girlfriends, because then I do care, then it starts to feel creepy and like . . . when *cousins* marry and maybe that's just the way I was brought up but I'm not the only person from our lives that feels that way, trust me . . .

GREG . . . then . . . I don't care . . .

STEPH Well, *that* part I do believe! That is the very first piece of truth that has come outta your mouth in the last ten minutes! "I don't care." (*Beat.*) No shit, Greg, I'm completely aware of that simple fact, you don't care about very much at all . . . about other people or the messes you make or . . . the *trail* of shit you leave behind!/ Fuck you, Greg, you fucking piece of . . . (*Hitting him.*) / FUCK!

GREG Steph, stop!/ Please, just . . . / Stop this!

He reaches out and grabs her by the shoulders. She shakes him off like his hands are on fire.

STEPH Don't you fucking touch me! Get off me!!/ You prick!!

GREG I'm not!/ I am not *touching* you!

STEPH Yes, you are! You put your fucking hands on my shoulders, what do you call *that*?!

GREG I'm trying to . . . / . . . just . . .

STEPH Stop it!/ Get off me, fuckhead!

GREG Steph, you stop it! Stop shouting!

STEPH Then quit holding onto me!

GREG I'm not! (GREG *lets go.*) See?! I am not anywhere near you, okay, so just stop! Stop the screaming thing!

STEPH I'M NOT SCREAMING!!

GREG Okay then!

STEPH Okay is right!! Shut the fuck up and back away from me!/ Further!!

GREG . . . Stephanie, just . . . / Stop it.

GREG *backs away, holding up his hands in mock surrender.*

STEPH Fuck off, Greg, don't pull your shit with me. I have got *zero* tolerance toward you and your bullshit ways now, so just fuck right off. You hear me?

GREG Yes, I hear you . . .

STEPH Yeah? Ya sure?

GREG Ummmm, yes, Steph, I do . . . *Helen Keller* could hear you, so I'm pretty sure that *I* can . . .

STEPH Who?!

GREG Nothing. No one.

STEPH You mean the little *blind* girl? Do you mean *that* Helen Keller?

GREG . . . yes . . .

STEPH Why the fuck would you bring her up now?! I really don't get you sometimes . . .

GREG Doesn't matter.

STEPH It does to me. When you say stupid shit it bothers me, especially when you think it's *smart* stupid shit . . . so go ahead and explain yourself. (*Beat.*) Go on. Make your point.

GREG She was deaf. That's why.

STEPH Helen Keller was *blind*, Greg.

GREG Yeah, I know, but she was deaf, too./ And dumb . . .

STEPH . . . no . . . / *What*?

GREG "Dumb." Meaning unable to speak . . . (*Beat.*) That's what they used to call it, before people made other people change it, to . . . like . . . (*Beat.*) They called it *dumb*.

STEPHANIE *looks at him, considering this. Still angry but now a little confused as well.* GREG *checks his groceries.*

STEPH Oh. (*Beat.*) Well, that's *dumb* . . . I mean, stupid.

GREG I know, but, that's what it is. They did used to say that.

STEPH Huh. Fine. Whatever. You were still trying to say something mean. To me./ *About* me.

GREG No, I wasn't . . . / . . . *uh-uh* . . .

STEPH Yeah, kinda. About me yelling so loud and all that shit . . .

GREG Well, I was just . . . you know . . .

STEPH Yeah, I do know, and it was mean.

GREG Ok, but . . . I wasn't trying to . . . nothing. I'm sorry.

STEPH Doesn't matter. You're just deflecting us on a particular subject. Your usual shit. Your typical "Greg" shit.

GREG No, that's . . . not . . .

STEPH And you're the one who's done something, not me. Let's just be totally clear about that . . . / You and Carly are the bad guys here so don't try to get out of it . . .

GREG Steph, stop./ We're not . . . "bad" . . .

STEPH Well, you're not being *nice*, let's put it that way, ok? Friends don't do that type of shit to each other, so you can call it whatever you want . . . but it's still pretty fucking shitty. Don't ya think?

GREG It's . . . no, I think it's . . . what *I* think is happening here is more like . . . ahhh . . . it's a "misunderstanding," Steph. That's all.

STEPH *Really*?

GREG Yeah. Kinda.

STEPH And which part am I not *understanding*? I heard you were fucking one of my friends, one of my best childhood girlfriends, so explain to me which part of that I'm not good at understanding. Please. Go ahead.

GREG . . . it just happened! This whole . . . Carly and I are, you know, we're seeing if it can work out and so we just . . . we hadn't told anybody yet. (*Beat.*) I think it's great, that we've . . . when two people are . . . trying to *connect* and, and *forge* . . . you know. Yeah.

STEPH Oh fuck.

GREG What?/ *Why*?

STEPH I hope you don't talk to her like that./ What a *load* of shit! I mean . . .

GREG . . . look, if you're just gonna be rude . . .

STEPH Your *usual* shit as well . . . it's not even, like, "good" shit.

GREG What the hell does that mean?

STEPH It means this: do you love her?

GREG . . . I'm not gonna get into . . . no./ *No*.

STEPH It's an easy question, Greg./ There's no in-between . . . I mean, unless you're some wishy-washy motherfucker. Like yourself. (*Beat.*) Are you in love with Carly?/ Tell me "yes" and I'll walk inside the store right now . . . last you'll ever see of me. Promise.

GREG *stops for a moment. Trying to decide what to say. He opens his mouth, stops. Re-groups, then tries again:*

GREG I don't have to answer that . . . / The feelings I have for her are . . . my own . . . and I don't need to share them with anyone. Not even you, Steph, no matter how loud you scream or, or, like, push me on this . . . (*Beat.*) I *know* this is hard for you . . . I understand. I've been dreading this moment and I knew it was coming, that I was gonna run into you somewhere and we'd have this *huge* . . . but you know what? Whatever. I can deal with it. I *am* dealing with it, right now.

STEPH Oh yeah, you're doing a *great* job.

GREG Just . . . (*Beat.*) Look . . . I'm sure it sucked to hear this from whoever told you . . . and that is *our* fault, Carly and me . . . but you can understand, too, right? She thinks the *world* of you and I didn't wanna be the one to just . . . doesn't that make sense? At all? It wasn't either of us wanting to deceive you . . . we've just both been *really* nervous to . . . to . . . you know?

STEPH Yeah. I know. (*Beat.*) But you still didn't answer my question, Greg.

GREG What?

STEPH Do you love her?

GREG . . . I don't know.

STEPH Just say it. If you do then you should be proud of it. *Happy* to say it. You hardly ever used to tell people about us when we were together . . . don't think I didn't notice . . . / Girls notice shit like that.

GREG What?/ That's not true.

STEPH No, yeah, it is. Some people didn't even know you *had* a girlfriend, even after we were together for, like, *four* years. That doesn't make anybody feel real secure . . .

GREG . . . but that's . . . not . . .

STEPH Think about it and you'll know that I'm telling the truth. You will . . . (*Beat.*) I don't know if you *ever* said it out loud, like, around our friends or anything. I mean, you hardly ever even said it to *me*!

GREG That's . . . I told you I loved you! Come on! (*Beat.*) You *know* I loved you. Stephanie.

STEPH No, I know you did, I'm just saying . . . this time around, make sure it's really obvious. / "Obvious" doesn't suck when it comes to love.

GREG Fine. / Ok then.

STEPH Okay.

GREG I'll . . . that's a good point.

STEPH It just . . . fuck . . . it blows my mind! It really does!

GREG I know, I know. It's . . . just . . .

STEPH I mean, somebody told me at work, over at the salon and it was, like, BAM!! Outta the blue and I felt this thing down in my stomach . . . this sorta . . . like somebody had dropped a piano on me. But from *inside*.

GREG I understand. (*Beat.*) I'm sure she wants to talk to you, too./ Yes. To explain.

STEPH Yeah?/ You think so?

GREG Of course. Carly's . . . just . . . you know . . .

STEPH "Nervous."

GREG A little bit.

STEPH Uh-huh. You said that.

STEPH *stands there, taking it all in.* GREG *glances inside his bag of groceries, worried about the frozen food.*

GREG I mean . . . can you understand that? Like, at least somewhat?

STEPH I guess.

GREG Good. So then . . . are we *cool*? (*Beat.*) Steph?

GREG *stops and waits, hoping for an answer.* STEPH *seems about to say something but stops. She points at his bag.*

STEPH . . . you're leaking.

GREG Oh. Shit. It's probably . . . the . . .

STEPH Here. Lemme see.

GREG . . . no, I can . . .

STEPH Just . . . (*Takes the bag.*) Give it.

STEPH *pulls out the box of ice cream sandwiches. Tosses it to the ground and smashes the shit out of it with her shoe. Again and again.*

STEPH . . . yeah, Greg. We're cool.

STEPH *turns and walks away without looking back.* GREG *is left standing alone with his crumpled bags of groceries.*

GREG (*To himself.*) Oh boy.

At work.

CARLY *sitting at the break room table, reading through an old magazine. Drinking a soda.*

She yawns and checks the clock. Almost the end of another shift. A loud buzzer goes off. Twice.

After a moment, the door opens and KENT *is standing there in the opening, wearing street clothes.*

CARLY *jumps to her feet, surprised. Oh shit.*

KENT . . . hey.

CARLY Kent.

KENT Hi.

CARLY Hello.

KENT So . . . this really is kinda strange, isn't it? Every time we . . . run into each other.

CARLY Ummmm, kinda. Yeah. (*Standing.*) Why're you here . . . *again*?

KENT I was just . . . they let me go a little bit early this morning . . . you guys needed a couple boxes of those thingies we use to close up the, ahhh . . . you know?/ The *clip*-thingies that they use for shipping those new whatever-you-call-'ems?

CARLY No./ I'm not sure.

KENT The . . . fucking . . . you *know*! (*Miming.*) iPads.

CARLY Oh yeah. Those.

KENT Yep. I guess people need 'em so they can *blog* and shit . . . (*Beat.*) I said I'd bring 'em over and so I just . . . you know . . . so I did that.

CARLY Ok.

KENT Thought I'd check to see if you're here.

CARLY You knew I was here. It's Thursday morning so you knew I'd be here. (*Beat.*) I'm the kind of person who *actually* goes where they say they're gonna go after telling someone where they'll be.

KENT Right.

CARLY Unlike you.

KENT Hey, come on . . .

CARLY No, *you* come on.

KENT Let's not fight. I'm only here for, like, *two* minutes.

CARLY Good.

CARLY *goes to the fridge. Gets an apple and takes a bite.*

KENT Jesus Christ. You gonna hate me forever?

CARLY I'm working on it. I feel like maybe at this rate . . . yeah . . . it's gonna be forever.

KENT Fine. I'm just trying to be nice here.

CARLY Two minutes goes fast. You got anything else to say?

KENT Fuck. No. (*Beat.*) Can I have some *coffee* before I leave?

CARLY I don't care. *I* didn't make it.

KENT I mean, it's company coffee. Just 'cause I'm over at the other plant, I should be able to have some when I'm on the clock.

CARLY Go for it, then. (*Starting to pack up.*) I need to get back up front . . .

KENT Why?

CARLY None of your business, that's why.

KENT I'm just asking.

CARLY Because it's the end of my shift, that's why. Because I have paperwork to finish and people to check on, ok? I'm a shift supervisor now with *increased* duties . . .

KENT . . . *God* . . . ok, ok . . .

CARLY Because *I* don't just stuff shit in boxes for a living, *that's* why. Do you fucking mind? I have responsibilities . . .

That one lands with KENT. *He turns quickly but manages to hold his temper—it's a struggle. You can tell.*

KENT Fine. Go.

CARLY I will. I'm going. (*Beat.*) Nice of you to ask about your *daughter* . . .

KENT Sorry, shit! I was gonna . . .

CARLY Yeah, I bet.

KENT I was *too*! Fuck, please, don't be like that, Carly! I'm trying here!

CARLY Ok, then go ahead. Ask something.

KENT Well . . . not *now*, I mean . . . (*Beat.*) Fine. How's the baby?

CARLY She's *three*.

KENT You *know* what I mean! Is she alright?

CARLY She's good. Great, actually.

KENT Yeah?

CARLY Yes, Kent. She's amazing—she looks like you, which I hate, but luckily you were always good-looking so it oughta be ok. (*Beat.*) You should ask to see her more . . . you might know some of this shit.

KENT . . . I thought you said . . . that . . .

CARLY No, I never said don't see her.

KENT Well, no, but . . .

CARLY That was never said. *Ever.* At some point you just stopped trying . . .

KENT It's hard. I mean, when . . . we're all . . .

CARLY Whatever. If picking up the phone is hard then yeah, it's hard. (*Checks the clock.*) I gotta go.

KENT . . . but . . .

CARLY Call me if you wanna spend some time with your daughter.

KENT I will.

CARLY We'll see.

CARLY *heads for the door.* KENT *calls out as she is going:*

KENT . . . is Greg picking you up?

CARLY *stops and turns to her ex. He is quiet but he seems to be a mixture of angry, sad and scared. Like a child.*

KENT Steph called me./ And she *never* calls me.

CARLY . . . *ok* . . . / So?

KENT Didn't you think that maybe you should tell me about this at some point?

CARLY I was gonna. At some point.

KENT Yeah? When's that?

CARLY . . . when it became anything close to being "your business."

KENT *Listen* . . . (*Stops himself.*) I'm trying hard not to go off here, ok? I have been doing a lot of work on me as a person—I don't mean in, like, some faggy way, but—I've really been trying lately to get hold of my anger and, and my . . . taking more of an *ownership* for my mistakes and shit like that. You haven't been around me at all but it's true. I'm doing that now . . .

CARLY Yeah?

KENT *Yes*. I even watched a *video* about it . . .

CARLY Great. (*Beat.*) I'll bet your little girlfriend Crystal is, like, *super* impressed with you . . .

KENT Carly, please, fuck! Just gimme a break here . . . *I'm* confronting *you* right now!

CARLY *Really*? Is that what you're doing?

KENT Yes! So come on . . . answer me! Seriously!

CARLY Alright. Fine. (*Beat.*) Yes, Kent, Greg is picking me up from work. He does that on occasion.

KENT . . . shit . . .

CARLY You know why? Because he's a gentleman, that's why. He does things for *me*, not just himself . . . he considers other people sometimes and even though he's gotta drive way outta town to where he's substitute teaching, he still does things like that . . . so think about *that* when you're over at *Dunkin' Donuts* this morning without a care in the world . . .

KENT Huh. (*Beat.*) So then . . . this has been going on for a while now, I guess.

CARLY Fuck you, Kent. That's all the answer a question like that deserves.

KENT *What*? You're doing the same thing I did to you . . . seeing somebody behind my back!

CARLY We were married, asshole! *Married*! That's totally different . . .

KENT He's my *friend*.

CARLY I wouldn't count on that in an *earthquake* if I were you . . .

KENT The *fuck* does that mean?

CARLY It means just how it sounds. (*Beat.*) I'm not sure you've *got* any friends, Kent . . .

KENT That's bullshit!

CARLY Well, I don't care, and that's the real answer. I'm tired and I need to get home to relieve my mom because Jennifer's had a fever the last couple nights . . .

KENT Really? I mean . . . is she . . . ?

CARLY She's fine. Don't pretend./ *You* stop.

KENT Oh stop./ I'm *asking*.

CARLY She's okay. I'm taking her in today but I think she's alright.

KENT That's . . . you need any money . . . or . . . ?

CARLY No. (*Yawns.*) I really need to go.

*They stand for a moment, facing each other, and then the worst thing that could happen does—*GREG *appears at the door, dressed in a shirt and tie. Looking in.*

They all remain frozen, like a Mexican stand-off directed by an Italian filmmaker. GREG *finally opens the door and enters the room.* CARLY *looks at* KENT, *then kisses* GREG. GREG *returns it, all the while keeping one eye on* KENT.

CARLY *turns and heads out the door. Calling back as she exits:*

CARLY . . . hey there./ I'll be back in a minute. I gotta finish up and punch out.

GREG Morning. Sorry if I'm . . . late./ Ok, that sounds good. I'll . . . just . . . (*Beat.*) Yeah.

The two men are left in the room alone. Sizing each other up in silence for a moment.

KENT I promised myself I wasn't gonna kill you if I saw you . . .

GREG I think that's a promise worth keeping.

KENT Yeah, but now I'm not so sure.

GREG . . . *Kent* . . .

KENT Forget it. I just hashed it out with her and I'm too fucking tired to get into it with you. At least this second . . .

GREG Great. Does that mean I can expect to get jumped one day in the parking lot or something? That should be fun for the kids . . .

KENT Maybe. Always worked for me before . . .

GREG *Look*, man . . . this is . . .

KENT Dude, no, I'm not gonna "look" or any of that shit. I don't need to be reasonable about this. This isn't one of your damn *novels*. She's my *wife*.

GREG *Ex*-wife, Kent.

KENT Whatever.

GREG No, not whatever. I'm not trying to start something here, but you lost her.

KENT Fuck that.

GREG You gave her up. *You* let that happen. Be honest, man. (*Beat*.) You know that's true.

KENT . . . Greg, you need to stop now . . .

GREG I'm not gonna fight with you, trust me, that's the last thing I want . . .

KENT Damn right. Don't think you'll be lucky and get in some *sucker-punch* now 'cause that shit just ain't gonna happen again.

GREG Kent, come on . . . let's just . . .

KENT People are talking behind my back, okay? *Laughing* at me . . .

GREG I'm sorry about that.

KENT I know I fucked up with her, I'm *aware* of that . . . and with you, too! I know that I'm a fucking douchebag sometimes! But Jesus, why'd you have to do *this*? Huh?

GREG . . . we didn't . . .

KENT All the girls in the world out there and you need to start in with my ex? I mean, that's, like, practically *incest*, dude!

GREG . . . ummmmmmm, not really, but . . .

KENT You know what I mean!

GREG Yeah, no, I do . . . (*Checks the clock.*) I've gotta do some work . . . I'm teaching English over at the middle school./ . . . *Subbing* . . .

KENT I know./ I heard from Carly.

GREG Ok. We're doing *Lord of the Flies* right now and I'm . . . I need to write a quiz.

KENT Oh. (*Beat.*) And that's it? "I gotta work" and you, just, like, turn your back on me?

GREG Well . . . sorta. Yeah. I mean . . .

KENT No apology, or . . . ?

GREG Right now?

KENT What, you wanna meet for *hot wings* and do it?

GREG Ummmmmm . . .

KENT Whatever, *bitch*.

GREG *is about to speak when* KENT *suddenly turns and bangs his boot against the door of the fridge. Denting it.*

KENT This sucks, man! Life just fucking *blows* sometimes . . .

GREG I know.

KENT I mean, all this shit with you two, and, and—(*Punches the fridge.*)—Goddamnit!!

GREG What?

KENT Nothing. Just stuff.

GREG No, man, what?

KENT *Nothing*. Don't worry about it. I wouldn't come to you with my problems, anyway . . . (*Beat.*) You better be fucking nice around my kid or I'll seriously go off on you . . . and I mean that.

GREG Come on.

KENT I'm not kidding. (*Beat.*) I'm not.

GREG *nods at this, fully realizing that* KENT *is not at all kidding. A long silence between them.*

GREG She's really cute, actually . . . Jennifer.

KENT Don't be gay.

GREG *What*?

KENT Everybody says she looks like me, so . . .

GREG Oh. Well, not to me she doesn't! She's a little *girl*, she's not a . . . forget it.

KENT (*Slamming his hand down on the counter.*) Fuck! I *hate* this!

GREG . . . dude . . .

KENT *Just* . . . (*Beat.*) I'm gonna go down and say "hi" to Rich and some of those other assholes so don't worry about me . . .

GREG Got it. (*Beat.*) You like it over there? At the Edgewater plant?

KENT It's fine. Same as here, except I'm back on nights. Only reason I left was so that Carly could keep her whole thing going . . .

GREG No, I know . . . and that was . . .

KENT Yeah, I know you know. You probably *know* everything now. Right?

GREG . . . no . . .

KENT . . . I suppose she's compared our cocks and all that crap that girls do! God, I can't fucking *stand* to even think about this . . .

GREG Come on, Kent, it's not . . .

KENT I *know* she has! She always told me about her other boyfriends and shit so obviously she has!/ *Measuring* us and getting all . . . fuck!!

GREG No, that's not . . . / She really hasn't!

KENT Whatever.

GREG . . . listen . . . Kent . . .

KENT Dude, I am just barely holding my shit together here, keeping myself from going after you with, like, *karate-chops*, so . . . you *need* to back off. 'Kay?/ I'm *serious*.

GREG . . . / Do what you gotta do, man.

This could get dangerous but just at the moment where one more word could ruin everything CARLY *appears at the door again.*

CARLY Hey. (*Beat.*) You ready?

GREG Yeah.

GREG *looks over at* KENT, *who remains poised.* GREG *starts to say something, then decides not to. He and* CARLY *exit.*

KENT *stands for a long time by himself. Looks like he's about to smash something but stops himself. Instead, he walks over to the shelf where the trophies of past softball victories stand and picks one up. Stares at it. Studying the little plastic figure that adorns the top.*

KENT (*To the trophy.*) . . . the fuck are *you* looking at, dickweed?

He calmly snaps the little player off the trophy and tosses it back onto the shelf.

He returns the trophy to its resting place and walks out. The break room door slams shut.

An outdoor lounge.

STEPHANIE *is sitting by herself, holding her keys. She is messing with her touch-screen phone.*

After a few moments, GREG *shows up. He's wearing a light sweater and trousers. Carrying a bag. He spots* STEPH *and goes to her. Sits.*

GREG . . . look at you with the fancy *gadget* there!

STEPH Yeah. Tim got me this phone so I was checking it out. He likes to go kinda *apeshit* on the apps, so I was . . . just . . .

They look at each other and then STEPH *reaches out for a hug. It goes well enough but it's a little bit awkward.*

GREG Anyway.

STEPH Thanks for meeting up./ During *work.*

GREG Sure./ 'Course. (*Beat.*) This used to be their "smoking porch," I guess, but the kids can't smoke at school now so they just call it "the porch." *Clever*, right?

STEPH Yep. (*Beat.*) Didn't know if you'd really wanna see me, but hey. I'm glad you did.

GREG Well, sounded urgent, so . . . I thought . . . I mean, last time was a little . . . you know . . . so I wasn't sure what to do . . . but yeah.

STEPH Well, I appreciate it. *(Beat.)* I've been trying to deal with things and, just . . . whatever. "Live and let live," I guess.

GREG That's good.

STEPH Still haven't talked to Carly but I'm not gonna chase her down in the street, so . . .

GREG You mean, like you did me . . . ?

STEPH (*Smiling.*) Asshole.

GREG . . . *kidding* . . . sort of.

STEPH She can't face me then it's her problem, I guess. Right?

GREG That's . . . (*Beat.*) I don't wanna get in the middle of it, so . . . you know.

STEPH I am not asking you to get *into* anything, Greg . . . I was looking for your opinion . . ./ Don't worry about it. We'll just figure it out at some other point. Her and me.

GREG Oh. (*Glancing around.*)/ Okay. I'm on my lunch, so we . . . should . . .

STEPH Nobody's *watching* us, alright?

GREG I *know*. I just . . . we're here at *school*, so that's a little . . . plus, it feels weird to be doing this. Meeting behind her back.

STEPH Why? We're just talking.

GREG Yeah, but . . .

STEPH You did it to me.

GREG Ummmm, no, that's not . . . true . . .

STEPH Yeah, you guys kept your whole *courtship* a secret, so . . . / Yes, you did.

GREG We didn't . . . no . . . / Steph, I'm not going to do this again, so *no*. Let's stop.

STEPH I'm not *fighting* with you! Fuck!! (*Beat.*) I asked you to come talk with me and it's not about you and Carly, so if you didn't tell her you were gonna see me, then that is your shit . . . run back to your *classroom* and hide if you wanna, I don't care!

GREG I'm not *running* anywhere! Jesus!! (*Beat.*) I just feel strange, that's all. Meeting like this. Plus it's the *student* lounge, so that's . . . anybody could just . . .

STEPH 'Kay. (*Beat.*) *Sorry*. I get it.

GREG What?

STEPH I said "sorry."

GREG I know . . . it's just so *rare*, I thought I misunderstood you. Do you mind saying it again, just once more? (*Smiles.*) Please?

STEPH "Fuck you." (*Smiles.*) I'll say *that* again for you if you'd like . . . a *dozen* times.

GREG *laughs and, in spite of herself, so does* STEPH. *She elbows him in the ribs.*

They stare off at kids playing in the distance.

GREG Look at 'em over there . . . at the *elementary* . . . kids are awesome, aren't they?

STEPH Yeah. Pretty much.

GREG Don't you think?

STEPH Mostly. (*Beat.*) I hate cutting their hair but yes, mostly they're pretty awesome . . .

GREG Ha! I'll bet they can be a handful!

STEPH Little fuckers, some of 'em, but it's the parents that're the *actual* problem.

GREG True.

STEPH Most children . . . I mean, if you track it back . . . it's the parents./ There's, like, a shitload of bad parents out there!

GREG No, yeah, I know . . ./ I see the same all the time here. I mean, I haven't been doing it very long, but . . . you're right. It's usually the adults.

STEPH Yep.

GREG Do you wanna sit? If we're gonna . . . then I need to eat.

STEPH Sure.

GREG . . . do you think you guys're gonna have any? (*Pointing*.) I mean, like, soon?

STEPH Oh, are we getting down to the *personal* shit now?

GREG Ha! Not really. Just a question.

STEPH I don't know. *He* wants to, but I'm not in a hurry./ Yet.

GREG Hmmm./ Always thought you wanted kids.

STEPH *shrugs and puts away her phone.* GREG *gets out a sandwich.*

STEPH I do. Just . . . not now. (*Beat*.) I think it's nice to just have a little time as a couple, before you get all . . . you know what I'm saying? "Tied down" or whatever.

GREG No, that's . . .

STEPH I don't know! I'm just talking.

GREG Big decision.

STEPH Shit yeah! They're all big decisions . . . after you hit twenty-one, every fucking time you turn around it's a big decision.

GREG True!

STEPH Marriage and kids and, and—the fact that we're considering going off to some other state. Rhode Island! (*Making a face*.) You ever think about living in *Rhode Island*? I mean, *where* the fuck is that?!

GREG Ha! Yeah. I did once.

STEPH Bullshit!

GREG No, I did, back in high school I did . . . when I was first looking at colleges I thought about it. Brown is up there.

STEPH "Brown?"/ That's the *name* of a college?

GREG Yeah./ Uh-huh. A good one, too.

STEPH "Brown" is the color of dog shit. What a stupid thing to call a school . . .

GREG Ha! Anyway . . . you guys might end up there?

STEPH I guess. Some tech company wants Tim to come run their . . . whatever-he-does . . .

GREG Great.

STEPH I suppose. (*Beat.*) All my family's here. He's got cousins in Boston, but mostly everybody's here, so I dunno.

GREG Well, I'm sure it'll work out . . .

STEPH Maybe. (*Beat.*) You think I should do it?

GREG I mean . . . if not, it's a helluva *commute*!

STEPH Right! (*Smiles.*) . . . *dick* . . .

GREG So, yeah, I guess. It's hard when couples have to make choices like that, but . . .

STEPH That's not what I'm asking you: "Should we do this?"/ I'm not asking that.

GREG Oh. Sorry./ Then I'm . . . what?

STEPH I'm saying "me." Should *I* go with him?

GREG Is that . . . even an *option*? For you? (*Beat.*) Steph?

STEPH It sounds like it's an option, doesn't it?

GREG Well . . . from what you're saying right at *this* moment, yeah . . . but . . .

STEPH So, yes, it's an option.

GREG Then you guys're . . . not . . . ? Are you happy? Steph?

STEPH We're fine. Like nine outta ten couples you meet. We're getting by.

GREG Got it.

STEPH I didn't come here to . . . but yeah. Tim's a totally nice guy, he's thoughtful and he does the dishes and shit. He'll watch my shows with me. (*Beat.*) Is that "happy?" I don't know. *He* seems fine with it . . .

GREG . . . but . . . you're . . . ?

STEPH I'm here, aren't I?

GREG I guess so.

STEPH Seeing you the other day, even though I was pissed and we got, you know . . . I was still aware of that *thing* between us. A connection. (*Beat.*) Was that just me, or am I fucking crazy?/ (*Grins.*) Don't answer that . . .

GREG Ummmmm . . . / *Steph.*

STEPH Ok. Tell me you didn't feel it then.

GREG It's not that I . . . *look* . . . shit . . .

STEPH Greg, please don't *prepare* an answer for me, alright? Just say the truth and I can live with that.

GREG Fine. It was nice to see you again, too.

STEPH Yeah?

GREG Even after you *murdered* my groceries . . . Yes. (*Beat.*) Is that what you wanna hear?

STEPH That's a start.

GREG Ok then. (*Checks his watch.*) It's almost time for fourth period./ I need to get . . .

STEPH Greg, fuck./ Can you give me another *five* minutes here . . . ? Is that possible?

GREG *gets to his feet. He isn't leaving but he's at least made the gesture.* STEPH *grabs hold of his arm.*

GREG Yeah, sure, I just . . . (*Sits.*) Go ahead.

STEPH Look . . . I walked away one time when that was the last thing I wanted to do, even though you said I should—and maybe you really *wanted* me to, I don't know—but I feel like you were *that* guy for me and I threw it away because it was easier to start over but that's all you do sometimes when you do that . . . you just start over, doing the same fucking thing you did before with some other man or woman or . . . you know? It's not some big magic trick and life is suddenly all *cotton candy* by changing partners. I was still me and, and, and here I am, only realizing that *now* . . .

GREG I understand what you're saying, Steph.

STEPH Yeah?/ You do?

GREG Absolutely./ Yes! It's *so* hard to *really* start again . . . I mean, I've just barely begun to do that myself.

STEPH I know, I know, and when I heard that—and it's not just because you're with Carly or anything, it's not—but when that news got to me and I was looking around at my own situation, I thought, "Fuck, he's with someone. It's *now* or never." I did. That was the phrase I heard in my head . . . "now or never."/ I mean, most people, we only get a few chances at this thing. *Love.* One or two goes at it, even it we're lucky.

GREG Yeah, but . . ./ I don't understand. What're you asking me here? To . . . just . . . ?

STEPH *looks over at* GREG, *then slides across to him—letting the gap between them slowly disappear.*

STEPH I think we should give it one more try. You and me.

GREG . . . *now*? Like . . . "us" now?

STEPH Yeah, Greg. I'm speaking of the present.

GREG Steph. *Stephanie*. That's . . . shit. *What*?

STEPH I miss you and I want you back. Please do not make me say this, like, *six* times . . .

GREG No, no, I'm just . . . I am trying to sort it all out in my head./ Because . . . it's . . .

STEPH I *know*./ I'm an idiot . . . I fucked this up. (*Softer now*.) You know it's good between us, Greg . . . when it's working, there is nothing like it./ (*Smiles*.) You *know* that.

GREG . . . yeah./ (*He touches her face*.) I know.

STEPH (*A little tearful*.) I miss you. I don't know how else to say it . . . I just fucking miss you. That's all.

GREG Me too. (*Beat*.) God! I never thought I'd be able to say those words out loud to anyone . . . especially you! But yeah. It's been a . . . *tough* . . . few years . . .

STEPH Totally.

GREG I started hanging out around Carly and we, you know . . . we had a couple laughs together and . . . without Kent there it just . . . we *clicked*. (*Beat*.) What would I even say to her? This is . . . she's a really sweet person and . . . I'm . . . oh, fuck. *Fuck*!

STEPH You gotta decide about that, Greg. (*Beat*.) I *honestly* am not doing this because of her . . . you believe that, right?

GREG I guess I do./ Steph . . .

STEPH No, tell me you *believe* that./ Say it.

GREG Ok. (*Beat*.) I *believe* you. But I'm still in a really bad spot . . . if we were to . . .

STEPH What?

GREG You know.

STEPH If we got back together?

GREG Yeah.

STEPH That's true. We both are.

GREG I gotta think about this . . .

STEPH You do?

GREG Steph, come on! You just dropped a *time bomb* in my lap here, so . . . you know?

STEPH I know. (*Beat.*) She's beautiful, right, so you need to think about it . . .

GREG No! It's not that.

STEPH Sure?

GREG That's never . . . been . . . *please* don't say something like that. That sounds bad.

STEPH No, I'm sorry. Shit. That was mean.

GREG Kinda.

STEPH Anyway, she's not *that* pretty! (*Laughs.*) God! Life is fucking nuts . . . *listen* to me!

GREG Honestly . . . it has nothing to do with that or anything about that . . . okay? (*Beat.*) Carly is a good person and I like her . . . you should know the truth about that. I've got real feelings for her, and, and . . . I *like* her, I do . . . I like her . . .

STEPH I get it. You *like* her.

GREG Yeah, she's . . . very . . . but yes, I haven't stopped thinking about you since you smashed my ice cream sandwiches into the pavement. (*Shaking his head.*) *Why* is that?

STEPH Maybe 'cause we're meant to be together.

GREG Could be.

STEPH Some shit outta one of those books you always have in your pocket . . . / (*Smiling.*) What're you reading these days?

GREG Ha!/ (*Taps his jacket.*) *Jailbird*. Vonnegut.

STEPH Why haven't I ever *heard* of any of these people?! These *novelists*?!/ That's so fucking strange to me!

GREG Because . . . / I'm an oddball.

STEPH No shit. You really are.

GREG Yep.

STEPH And yet . . . somehow . . . I still like you.

GREG I know.

STEPH Yeah, well, don't get all cocky about it.

GREG Gotcha.

STEPH . . . and me? What about me, Greg?

GREG What?

STEPH You still like me? After all this time?

GREG Yeah, Steph. I do. I still like you . . .

GREG *glances around—checking for students—then slowly he and* STEPHANIE *kiss. Bodies tangling together.*

There's nothing tentative about it. It just keeps growing and growing and growing.

At work.

GREG *sitting in the break room. Early morning and he is dressed for teaching.*

He gets up and checks his watch a few times. Pulls out a book to read, tries to focus, stops. Replaces it. Yawns.

The door opens and KENT *walks in wearing street clothes—he carries a carton of paper towels. Drops it. Silence.*

KENT . . . oh.

GREG Hey, Kent.

KENT Greg.

GREG Geez . . . you're back here more than *I* am.

KENT I fucking *hope* so.

GREG . . . that was meant to be a *joke* . . .

KENT Ok. (*Beat.*) I mean, I'm still an employee. Not "here" but for the same people . . .

GREG Right.

KENT They have me do a lot of deliveries and stuff. I know the plant and so you don't have to explain it, like, *forty* times in *Mexican* to some dude if I just go do it.

GREG *chuckles at this, trying to keep it light.* KENT *does as well. It's a start.*

GREG . . . makes sense.

KENT Yep. Plus I usually get to leave early that way, which I don't hate . . .

GREG Gets you back home to Crystal, right?

KENT Uh-huh. (*Beat.*) So, you're picking Carly up, I s'ppose?

GREG Yeah. Her car's been acting up, so . . .

KENT Really? She didn't tell me that. Not that I just saw her—I didn't today, I didn't even ask where she was—but she usually tells me about stuff like that. (*Beat.*) What, you think we don't talk now?

GREG I don't think about it too much at all.

KENT Whatever.

GREG Kent, I'm not . . . I'm just saying that's your business. Yours and hers.

KENT Fuck, you should work in an *embassy* or something. You're *so* diplomatic. (*Beat.*) Is that the right word?

GREG Yep. It is.

KENT Anyways . . . yeah, if something goes wrong with her car or at the duplex, that sorta thing, I tend to hear about it.

GREG Ok by me./ Yep.

KENT Great./ Super.

GREG You should let her know, then. I'm sure she'd appreciate it . . .

KENT She's got my number. If it's bad she'll call./ *Trust* me . . .

GREG Ok./ Fine.

They wander off this topic and stand around for a minute.

KENT . . . you miss it here? Nights?

GREG Sometimes.

KENT You *do*?

GREG Yeah! Once in a while—we had some good times./ Every so often.

KENT I guess./ Right.

GREG . . . come on . . .

KENT A couple, maybe.

GREG More than that. (*Beat.*) Remember the night we locked that new foreman in the freezer for, like, an *hour*?/ 'Member that?

KENT Oh shit!/ Yes . . .

GREG That guy was SO pissed, but Rich covered the cameras and so they could . . . never . . .

KENT I heard he had *frostbite* on his pubes when he came outta there or something! Seriously!

GREG No!/ What?!

KENT Yes!/ Like dangling ice crystals! Fuck!!

They laugh at this. Guys laugh at the dumbest shit so it really isn't a surprise. After a minute, they stop.

GREG . . . and speaking of "crystal" . . .

KENT Dude, stop./ Not funny.

GREG What?/ I was just gonna ask . . . if . . .

KENT Don't go there. (*Beat.*) My life is none of your business any more./ Off-limits.

GREG *Sorry.*/ I wasn't . . . trying to . . .

KENT Don't worry about it. (*Checks his watch.*) I should go.

GREG Ok then.

KENT Tell Carly to ring me up if her car keeps giving her grief . . . she probably needs to get the oil changed is all . . . I tell her that all the time but she never listens to me.

GREG No, actually, I tried that. I changed it over the weekend.

KENT Yeah?

GREG Yep, so it's not that . . .

KENT *You* did it, or you had it changed?

GREG What's the difference?

KENT I just can't picture you crawling under a car and working down there. That's all.

GREG Fine. Yes, I had it done at Jiffy-Lube.

KENT Ok. That sounds more like it. (*Beat.*) So if she calls me I'll check it out . . .

GREG Cool.

KENT Alright, see ya around, I guess. (*Starts off.*) You think Steph ever cheated on you?

GREG . . . *Kent* . . .

KENT I'm just asking.

GREG Are we really gonna keep doing this? *Picking* at each other, because . . . I'm . . .

KENT This has nothing to do with that! Fuck, just *listen* to me, okay?!! (*Beat.*) I am honestly asking you a question here . . .

GREG Fine. No, I don't think so.

KENT Yeah?

GREG I'm almost sure "no."

KENT And I'm not doubting that, I just asked you is all . . . (*Beat.*) But why are you *so* sure she didn't? Huh?

GREG It's . . . just a feeling. Since it never crossed my mind, *ever*, I guess I just feel secure about it . . .

KENT Yeah, I s'ppose you mostly only worry if it's a pretty girl. Right?/ I mean . . .

GREG . . . *dude* . . . / That is *not* cool . . .

KENT You *know* what I'm saying! I'm . . . (*Beat.*) I think Crystal's fucking around on me.

GREG What?

KENT Maybe.

GREG *Really*?

KENT She's so hot, I mean . . . every guy we walk by looks at her—stares—and I am *right* there!/ It's fucking unbelievable!

GREG That sucks./ Damn.

KENT Yeah, but I mean . . . I am *next* to her! And I'm a decent-sized guy, athletic, they've gotta know they're taking a chance but it still happens, *all* the time! Constantly! (*Beat.*) And she fucking loves it, I mean, the *attention* like that? Completely eats it up, and I don't say anything, we keep moving on, we're living together . . . but something has been gnawing at me for a little while now. Just things. Back on nights so it's impossible to know what she's up to . . . always off running around with her friends . . . so I just thought I'd ask. Whatever. (*Beat.*) It's my problem.

KENT *shrugs and kicks at the table for a beat. Waiting.*

GREG . . . shit.

KENT I'll figure it out. I just thought you might've dealt with it before . . .

GREG Not really.

KENT I know what you mean. As beautiful as Carly is . . . I never felt that fear. Not once . . . (*Beat.*) *I* was the asshole in our marriage, not her.

GREG Well, that's . . . very . . . honest. You should feel good about that.

KENT Thanks, *Dr. Phil*. (*Beat.*) Don't be such a fag, ok? I was just asking . . . (*Beat.*) And keep this stuff to yourself.

GREG Of course. (*Beat.*) So, is that why you're volunteering for crap like this, running over here and . . . so you can sneak home at odd hours . . . or . . . ?

KENT Look at you! I knew all that reading was gonna pay off big for you one day!

GREG *And* . . . ?/ Come on, man, what's going on?

KENT Don't worry about it./ I gotta go. (*Looks at* GREG'*s book.*) *White Fang.* Sounds gay.

GREG But, no, hey . . . seriously . . . Kent . . .

KENT What?

GREG If you . . . I dunno . . . if you need somebody to, like, you know . . . / Something.

KENT What?/ *Spy* on her for me?

GREG Whatever. I'm not sure—to just help out.

KENT Nah, man, that's okay . . . you're kind of a girl when it comes to shit like that. *The going gets tough* and that sorta thing . . .

GREG Fine. I just thought I could . . . maybe if you needed a *friend* . . . or . . .

KENT I do. I absolutely do. I'm in *real* need of a fucking friend right about now . . .

GREG . . . ok . . .

KENT . . . but I do not need *you*. Sorry, dude.

GREG I understand.

KENT *shrugs and heads out the door.* GREG *turns to look at a nearby clock. One of those buzzers breaks the silence.*

Not much later CARLY *enters out of uniform—lunch pail and purse in one hand. She moves to* GREG *and kisses him.*

CARLY . . . ahhh, "freedom!"

GREG Ha! Couldn't wait, huh? To get outta the uniform?/ (*Kisses her.*) Morning.

CARLY Nope!/ Good morning . . . thanks for coming again, I promise I'm gonna check on the car today. (*Smiles.*) Or *tomorrow*.

GREG Whenever is fine. It's easy for me to get you so it's not a problem . . .

CARLY Great. You ready?

GREG Sure. I've got a little time . . . you wanna go get breakfast at the IHOP . . . or . . . ?

CARLY Ummmmm . . . I'm alright, unless you want to./ I can *always* eat pancakes, but . . . (*Beat.*) It's up to you.

GREG I'm fine./ I was just . . . thought it'd be nice to have some food and just talk. It's hard sometimes . . . with Jennifer and . . . / Our . . . schedules, so, you know . . .

CARLY No, I agree . . . / It's a good idea. (*Beat.*) *Lots* to talk about?

GREG Ummmmm, no . . . just stuff, "us" stuff . . . I like being with you and I figured, since I have first period open today, why not?

CARLY Good. Let's go for it. (*Kisses him.*) Maybe we can go back to the house for a little while after since Mom's got Jennifer.

GREG . . . sure . . .

CARLY Don't ya think? She usually lets me sleep for a few hours before she drops her off, so . . . let's . . .

GREG Yeah, we can . . . do you wanna do that now? I mean, instead?

CARLY We could.

GREG That's . . .

CARLY Or we could do the pancakes first. They both sound good!

GREG Ha! I'm open . . . (*Checks his watch.*) For another two hours, anyway.

CARLY Food! I need something yummy to eat . . .

GREG 'Kay, let's take care of that right now.

CARLY Fantastic! (*Grabbing him.*) You know what? You're a really good guy, Greg./ I think you are a *really* decent and nice person and I'm glad that we're together now . . . so . . . there you go.

GREG Thank you./ (*A peck on her cheek.*) That is very sweet. Thanks.

CARLY You *definitely* need pancakes first! (*She laughs.*) I thought that was gonna get you all hot and bothered when I said that . . .

GREG Ha! This might not be the most . . . *sexy* . . . place I've ever been before, so maybe . . .

They kiss a few more times. It grows in intensity until:

CARLY You know what? Fuck the pancakes. Let's go to your place and I'm gonna eat *you* for breakfast . . .

GREG Ha!/ Come on, let's go to IHOP . . .

CARLY No, seriously . . . / I feel really horny right now, so we should . . . come on.

GREG Carly, that's . . .

CARLY . . . *please*, baby . . .

GREG No, really, I've got a test to finish up and a . . . *seating chart* I'm supposed to . . .

CARLY Excuse me?

GREG What?

CARLY Nothing.

GREG No, what'd I do wrong?

CARLY Ummmmmm . . . it started with "seating" and it ended with "chart."

GREG I do, though! For my . . . the teacher I'm subbing for asked me to . . .

CARLY Screw it, Greg, I can *walk* home if you've gotta get over there *that* bad.

GREG After breakfast is fine . . . I'm just . . .

CARLY I was saying I wanna blow you, Greg, to suck your cock . . .

so can you hold off on the *Elmer's Glue Stick* for a few minutes or not?/ I mean . . . God!

GREG Carly, come on . . . / That's . . . not . . .

CARLY No, seriously, what's up? You're giving off some really mixed signals here . . .

GREG I have to be at work, that's all! I *want* to spend time with you, that's why I was here at 6:00 in the morning. Okay? There is nothing *wrong*, I promise . . .

CARLY . . . fine . . .

CARLY *moves away from* GREG. *He tries to get close to her.*

GREG Please. Don't get all . . .

CARLY Don't worry, I won't *hit* you or anything. Like your last relationship.

GREG That's not very nice.

CARLY I wasn't trying to be nice.

GREG We can go to my apartment if you want to. We absolutely can . . . I'm sorry.

CARLY Not now. (*Beat*.) It's ok . . . let's go eat.

GREG Good. Alright. You're sure?

CARLY Yeah, that's . . . yes. You said it'd be a fun thing to do and you're right. Sit and eat and talk, that sounds good . . .

GREG It will be.

CARLY Anything special you wanna talk about?

GREG . . . no . . .

CARLY Sure?

GREG No, I just . . . time together is what I was looking for./ That's all. *Promise*.

CARLY Cool./ Me too.

GREG Alright, then. You wanna wait here and I'll bring the car around, or . . . ?

CARLY No, I can walk with you. (*Smiles.*) Feels so good to get that uniform off in the morning, you know?/ Damn *polyester*!

GREG Yeah./ I used to peel my overalls off in the *bathroom* here, second I was done . . .

CARLY Graveyard shift is making me look *old*!

GREG Not possible! You're *so* beautiful . . .

CARLY Hmmmm . . . I like the way you make up.

GREG Ha! You know it's true . . .

CARLY No I don't. I never felt that.

GREG Really? "Never?" Come on!

CARLY Not so much. I mean, I could tell that other people would look at me and smile or watch me or . . . that kinda thing . . . but I didn't see anything special when I looked in the mirror./ Honestly. To this day.

GREG Huh./ Well, *I* do. (*Beat.*) You're great.

CARLY Thanks, baby.

GREG I'm just telling the truth, that's all.

CARLY You might still get that blow job . . . / *If* you keep working on it.

GREG Good./ I'll . . . *compliments* on the way! (*He kisses her.*) Come on, let's get going . . .

They start off but CARLY *stops* GREG. *Looks into his eyes.*

CARLY You know what . . . ? (*Pulls him closer.*) You make me feel safe. Did you know that?

GREG . . . that's . . .

CARLY I never felt that before, with a guy. I mean . . . you know,

I've been in love and, like, felt sexy or wanted someone, all of that stuff, but with you I feel *safe*. It's different. And it's nice.

GREG Thank you . . . that's . . . you too! It feels really nice to be around you. Too.

CARLY I hope so.

*A moment between them—*GREG *realizes now is the time to speak up and so he gives it a try:*

GREG Listen . . . Carly . . . I wanna say something . . . I *need* to say this to you and so I'm just going to . . . I am . . . right now . . .

CARLY No, me first./ Girls go first, right?

GREG Of course./ (*He does a little bow.*) Yes.

CARLY You sure?

GREG Please. Go ahead . . . I can wait.

CARLY This morning . . . I was . . . maybe we should go to breakfast and we can talk there. Want to?

GREG No, that's ok, we can . . . what?

CARLY I just . . . the last couple days, I've been all . . . anyway, I brought a test with me . . . you're supposed to do a clean catch for a pure reading but I've been working, so I thought, "what the hell, I'll at least try it first thing in the morning." When I'm getting done with my shift, right?

GREG . . . I don't understand./ Wait, like a . . . ?

CARLY I did it in the bathroom./ Just now. (*She pulls the stick out of her purse.*) We're gonna have a baby, Greg. You and me.

GREG . . . oh my God./ Wow. Carly . . . that's . . .

CARLY I *know*, right?/ Fuck, I can't believe it! (*Smiles.*) I hope you're happy . . .

GREG Of course. Yes. I mean . . . are *you* happy?

Without waiting for any more explanation, CARLY *grabs him and hugs him deeply. He holds her, unsure what else to do at this moment.*

Finally she pulls away, handing him the pregnancy strip to look at while she gathers her belongings.

CARLY And what were you gonna say to me?/ I mean before I cut you off . . . ?

GREG . . . nothing./ I was . . . I can't remember now.

CARLY *hugs him again and* GREG *hugs her back. Her eyes are closed but his are wide open—he stares at the used pregnancy test in his hand.*

A restaurant patio.

STEPH *and* GREG *outside.* GREG *holding a restaurant pager and looking at a nearby window.* STEPH *is watching him.*

STEPH . . . hey. You like my dress?/ I bought it for tonight. Special.

GREG Yes . . . it's really cute./ (*Beat.*) Wait, you're trying to trick me . . . that's a *skirt*, right, not a . . .? With a top.

STEPH A blouse.

GREG A blouse. *On* top.

STEPH Actually, yeah./ (*Smiles.*) Good job!

GREG I remember . . . / You taught me that. Yep.

GREG *smiles and turns away.* STEPH *keeps an eye on him.*

STEPH . . . you don't really wanna be here, do you?/ *Greg.*

GREG . . . / What?

STEPH It's true.

GREG Steph.

STEPH No, I can tell. It's alright, just say so.

GREG I'm . . . (*Turns to her.*) I'm sorry, I was just thinking, that's all.

STEPH That's ok. Thinking's allowed.

GREG Thanks.

STEPH As long as it's about "me." (*Smiles.*) I hope it was, anyway.

GREG Yeah, no, it was. Mostly about you and, you know. *Us.*

STEPH Uh-oh.

GREG No, no, there's no "uh-oh," I'm just . . . I've got lots of stuff going on, racing around in my head. (*Grins.*) Sorry. I've been looking forward to this, so . . .

STEPH Good. Me too.

GREG Great.

STEPH This restaurant looks nice . . . *busy*, but . . .

GREG Yeah, another one of those places that we always said we were gonna try and didn't. (*Beat.*) After we broke up, I never really wanted to go by myself—even if we never went there—if we'd *talked* about it then it felt like it was one of "our" spots so I didn't wanna ruin it. Does that at all make sense? (*Beat.*) NO! It's weird, right?

STEPH No, I get it./ That's sweet.

GREG Yeah?/ Thanks.

STEPH (*Looking around.*) I don't think I've even done *Turkish* in my life before, so . . . what kinda stuff is it?/ *Hummus*?

GREG Ummmm, you know . . . / Yeah. Kebobs and that kind of thing, too. *Mint*.

STEPH Like, "shish kebobs," you mean?

GREG Yep, like on . . . (*Mimes.*) . . . a stick. They probably don't use actual *sticks*, but . . . it's the same idea.

STEPH Right. Ok. Sounds . . . European. Or Asian. Which one are they?/ People from Turkey?

GREG Ahhhh, they're . . . / Technically neither, I think. It's Asia *Minor*. Or *Anatolia*.

STEPH Huh. 'Cause they're right down there on a map where it gets . . . all . . . *messy*. Right?/ At the bottom, by . . . (*Miming.*) . . . the . . .

GREG Ha!/ Yeah, down by all those countries that're . . . it's a *jumble* down there!

STEPH I know! Fuck, I used to hate Geography. In school. *Hated* that shit . . . (*Beat.*) We live in America, for God's sake, who gives a shit where the *straits* of Gibraltar are . . . right?

GREG Yeah. Absolutely. (*Beat.*) I think there's just *one* of 'em, but yes. I agree.

STEPH One what?

GREG Doesn't matter. (*Beat.*) Should I check on our . . . with the hostess?

STEPH Nah, it's ok. I don't mind waiting. It's nice out. (*She points.*) Why don't we just sit until the little thingie buzzes?

GREG 'Kay.

They wander over to a bench and take a seat. They hold hands. GREG *studies the buzzer. Shakes it. Waits.*

STEPH Where are you supposed to be instead?

GREG What?

STEPH Instead of at dinner? With me?

GREG . . .

STEPH Obviously you didn't tell Carly yet, so I'm just curious./ Where?

GREG Ummmm . . . / At a school thing. I *was* there, actually, just before this, so . . . / It's not a *complete* lie . . . because of . . .

STEPH I see./ That's great.

GREG I just . . . but no, I didn't tell her yet. About us.

GREG *starts to say something else but stops. He shrugs.*

STEPH Then how come we're doing this?/ Why?

GREG Huh?/ What's that mean?

STEPH I mean I don't wanna keep sneaking around like some . . . *fucking* . . .

GREG . . . I know, I know . . . !

STEPH Well, then do something about it, Greg.

GREG I'm trying to! It's not so easy . . .

STEPH Ummmmm, it should be./ Yeah.

GREG Really?/ Why's that?

STEPH Because you wanna be with me! Or so you said . . .

GREG . . . you *know* I do, that is not the issue here, alright?

STEPH Then enlighten me. (*Beat.*) And *real* fucking quickly, too, if you don't mind . . .

GREG I'm trying to.

STEPH *Trying* is bullshit; you either do something or you don't . . . it's that simple.

GREG . . . it . . . hasn't been very long . . . yet . . .

STEPH Long enough for me to walk out on Tim! For me to pack up my shit and move back to my parents' house and have the two of them look at me across the table like I'm a fucking crazy person—they *like* Tim. I think they like him more than they like me!—but I've done *all* that already, and *I* was married!! I have to go through a divorce and watch everybody around here staring at me or, or, or smiling behind my back, figuring that I wasn't good enough for him . . . that kinda shit . . . but *I* did it and I'm willing to live with that for you. For *you*, Greg. And part of that was because you made it clear—or as clear as anything that you ever do, which is pretty much like the consistency of "mud"—that you felt the same way as me. That you were in need of me back in your life. (*Beat.*) *That* is how long it's been by my count . . . so . . .

GREG Ok, fine. Point made./ Jesus.

STEPH I'm not trying to make any points here./ Or *win* any points or anything like that, I'm just saying that we need to *do* this if it's actually gonna happen . . .

GREG . . . I *know* . . .

STEPH I wanna be with you, I really do, and I feel like I've proved that to you. Done what it takes to show you that I'm not just fucking around here./ (*Beat.*) I love you.

GREG I know that!/ I see what you're . . . I know *exactly* what you've done and it's great, you're a really . . . big . . . inspiration . . .

STEPH *Inspiration*? Are you fucking kidding me?!

GREG No, I'm trying to articulate my thoughts here, so . . .

STEPH Just do it! You're not doing her a favor by dragging it out, you know *that* . . .

GREG No, I realize that, but . . .

STEPH I'm serious. She doesn't deserve that, I mean, nobody does . . . you need to do it now before we go any further here. I mean it.

GREG Steph, I'm going to! I *am* . . . I just need to find the . . . you know . . . the right time.

STEPH *Now*! Today! (*Looks at her watch.*) There's no special holiday coming up or anything like that . . . October isn't "break the news to a loved one" month so there's no need to wait, Greg. (*Beat.*) You've just gotta suck it up and talk to her. *Please.*/ Just do it and get it over with . . .

GREG I will./ *Okay.*

STEPH I'm completely being serious here.

GREG I know, Steph. (*Looks at her.*) I know your serious face, so . . . yeah. I-get-it.

STEPH Good . . . (*Beat.*) Unless you're telling me that what I've done was for nothing—and yes, I'm *aware* that I wasn't sure about how things were going in my marriage but you know I never would've done this without an indication from you that this is what you wanted, too!/ You *know* that!

GREG Steph, I *do* want this./ I want you. (*Beat.*) I promise.

STEPH Thank you . . . but a promise isn't enough. I know how you can be . . . dragging your feet and shit . . . it was murder getting you just to pay the *water bill* back in the day so forgive me if I have doubts on how long "breaking up" with someone is gonna take!

GREG Stop! (*Beat.*) Please. I'm gonna do it but it needs to be my way, alright? I didn't ask you to run home and tell Tim it was over . . . nobody *forced* you to do it, so . . . lemme just . . . have . . .

STEPH But you *wanted* me to, right?/ Didn't you?

GREG Yes!/ I fully expected that you . . . were . . . at *some* point, yeah, I did . . . but . . .

STEPH Greg!/ Fuck! You're scaring me here!

GREG What?!/ Stop, we're out in public . . . .

STEPH I don't care! Honestly, I don't even feel hungry now!/ God-damnit! FUCK!!

GREG Stephanie, stop it./ *Please* stop!

GREG *puts an arm around and she starts to throw it off but he holds on. They tussle but she gives in. She lets him comfort her, even though she's not very happy about it.*

STEPH Well . . . I don't understand what you're saying to me here but the sound of it sucks. I don't like it . . . at *all*.

GREG I'm just *saying* . . . I need a little bit of time. I'm not you, I don't do things with the exact same . . . *velocity* that you do but that doesn't make it bad or wrong or, or like I'm not gonna do it . . . so, come on.

STEPH Fine.

GREG Thank you.

STEPH But *soon*, alright?

GREG Yes. Of course.

STEPH No, I mean it. (*Beat.*) Please don't make me go talk to her, 'cause I will . . .

GREG Steph, don't say that.

STEPH Well, then just go do it./ When?

GREG I'm gonna!/ STOP! I'm working on it . . .

GREG *wants this conversation to be over—he stands up and looks off toward the front door of the restaurant. Checks the buzzer.*

STEPH That thing's not gonna save you, Greg . . . I'm right here so you might as well talk to me.

GREG I know that. I'm just hungry./ I *am*!

STEPH Sure./ Ok, alright. You're hungry.

STEPH *turns to* GREG, *takes the buzzer out of his hand and forces him to concentrate.*

GREG What're we doing now? What is this?

STEPH I just want you to focus, so I'm . . . here. Look at me./ In the *eye*, Greg.

GREG Fine./ I *am*.

STEPH Give me five good reasons that you want to be here. Today. With *me*.

GREG What?

STEPH Seriously . . . don't think about it, just do it.

GREG Why do we have to play this game, Steph?

STEPH It's not a game, I'm just asking you to.

GREG Fine . . . (*Beat.*) I just don't see why you need to . . . but fine. Ok. (*Beat.*) Five?

STEPH I could do it in two seconds . . .

GREG No, you couldn't.

STEPH Yes! It's easy.

GREG Do it, then.

STEPH Yeah, *sure*, so you can get out of it!

GREG That's not why!

STEPH Bullshit . . . .

GREG No, I said that because you were rubbing it in my face, so I was . . . just . . .

STEPH One. Because I'm hungry . . .

GREG Oh. Nice. *That's* romantic.

STEPH Shhh! My turn first. You wanted me to go, so here I am, I'm going, now be quiet and listen. One. Because I'm hungry . . . Two. I am an adventurous eater so I look forward to the challenge of whatever the fuck it is they eat in *Turkey*. Three. I can't eat another one of those roasted chickens that my mother brings home from the store without having to seriously take a *chainsaw* to my whole family, so that's . . . (*She mimes this*.) Four. I'm super fucking in love with you, Greg, and I wanna be around you every chance I get, and ta-da-da-dah! Five. I *love* you. I really do love you and so, yeah, it's worth saying again, so there it is. I-love-you. (*Beat*.) Those are *my* five. What about you?

GREG I'm sorry, what were the last two?/ Did I miss those? I think I nodded off at . . .

STEPH Fucker!/ (*Slugs him in the arm*.) Be serious!

GREG Fine! Okay . . . (*Rubs his arm*.) Owww. Jesus, you pack a wallop . . .

STEPH I have brothers.

GREG I know . . . but still.

STEPH Stop deflecting./ *Go*.

GREG Fine./ (*Beat.*) Five in total, right?

STEPH You're such a prick sometimes . . .

GREG What? I'm just *playing* around . . .

STEPH Then do it./ Just say 'em, come on.

GREG Alright, alright./ Top five. Ok, my very toppest-five reasons to be here with you, Steph, are . . . ummmm . . . ummmmmmmmmmm . . .

STEPH . . . *nice* . . .

GREG I'm just being silly! (*Smiles.*) Ok, honestly: I, too, like food, so I'm gonna share that one with you, the "food" one . . . two, I'm obviously the only person here who has any idea where *Turkey* is . . ./ . . . so really I'm more like your travel guide than a date or anything . . .

STEPH . . . shut up . . . / Asshole . . .

GREG You know that's true! Three would be . . . three is I'm definitely not going to be invited to eat at your parents' house at any point in the next, ohhh, say, *seven* years so we have to eat somewhere . . . and four is . . . hmmmmm . . . four would be . . . God, there must be at least *one* more reason . . .

STEPH You're such a dick, you know that? (*She smacks him on the shoulder.*) Say it!

GREG Alright, alright . . . (*The buzzer goes off.*) Ohh, damn, well . . . maybe by the time we're having dessert I'll've come up with . . .

STEPH No way! No! Say it *now*!!

*They are being playful with each other—*GREG *gets to his feet, pretending to head inside but* STEPH *has grabbed his arm and is pulling him back.*

After a moment, they kiss. Nothing big, just softly and tenderly—they're a nice couple when they work at it.

GREG Ok, you win. (*Beat.*) I love you, Steph. *That's* why. And I wanna be with you . . .

STEPH Thank you.

GREG Now let's go eat some . . . *stuff* on a stick.

STEPH Wait! No . . . no, no, no./ Not yet!

GREG But the . . . what's-it is buzzing!/ They're calling for us . . .

STEPH Fuck them, they can wait. They're Asian, they're used to waiting . . .

GREG . . . I don't even know what that means . . .

STEPH Shut up, I'm being serious! (*Beat.*) That's only four . . . *four* reasons to be here with me. What's the other one, your last one?/ No, tell me first. And be *truthful*.

GREG But . . . our little buzzer . . . / Damn! Fine. Lemme see . . . ok: (*Suddenly more serious.*) I'm happy to be here with you and *not* at some dinner with Carly when she starts crying because of what I've *allowed* to let happen. (*Beat.*) *There*. That's my last one.

STEPH Oh./ Okay.

GREG See?/ Number five wasn't so great, was it?

STEPH Ummmmm, no . . . maybe not as good as those other four. No.

GREG Well . . . you asked me to be truthful, so . . .

STEPH . . . yeah, but . . .

GREG Sorry.

STEPH No. Whatever. At least it was honest.

GREG Yeah.

GREG *sighs and looks away. He shrugs.* STEPH *watches him.*

STEPH . . . what does that mean? A "shrug?"

GREG It means I don't know what the hell to do right now, Steph. It means Carly . . . well, not just her, but . . . Carly and I . . . *we* . . . / She's . . . *shit* . . . she's pregnant.

STEPH *What*?/ . . . excuse me?

GREG . . . I'm . . . just . . . yeah. (*Beat.*) She is.

STEPH I hope to God you're not trying to be at all funny right now . . .

GREG Are you laughing?

STEPH That's . . . so . . . you got her pregnant?/ Is it . . . for sure?

GREG Yes./ I'm sorry, Steph. I'm just . . . really, really sorry.

STEPH Oh. God./ Shit./ *Fuck*.

GREG I know./ Yeah./ Kinda.

STEPH *stares at* GREG*—it's a mix of anger and pity and sadness.* GREG *stands there, shoulders hunched. His head bowed and his eyes closed.*

STEPH *can't help herself. She goes to him and allows him to put his head on her shoulder.*

The buzzer goes off again. STEPH *takes a deep breath, then grabs* GREG *by the hand. Pulls him close and says:*

STEPH . . . come on. Let's go eat.

Neither one of them gets to their feet. They sit on the bench, huddled together. The pager continues to blink and buzz.

At work.

CARLY *sitting at the table. Staring at* GREG, *who stands holding cups of coffee. A book under one arm. Silence.*

CARLY . . . you should talk now.

GREG . . .

CARLY I mean, you're here where you don't work when I don't need you to pick me up . . . so that's, you know . . . probably not the best sign in the world.

GREG Ummm . . . I just . . . wanted to *see* you. (*Pulls a bag out of his coat.*) And *look*: brought you a cinnamon roll, too . . . so . . .

She motions for GREG *to sit. He hesitates but then does.*

CARLY Just say it. (*Beat.*) And to help you get going . . . I already know . . . / *Greg* . . . come on . . .

GREG What?/ No, wait . . . what're you . . . ?

CARLY I know the *truth*. (*Beat.*) Even though we haven't talked in, like, however long . . . Steph had the decency to call me.

GREG *Steph* called you? When?

CARLY Whenever. A few days ago./ A week, maybe.

GREG Wait . . . / So, then . . . you've just been . . .

CARLY I was waiting for you! (*Beat.*) You told her about the baby, so it makes sense—I think she got scared and . . . anyway, she called and we met up. We talked it out.

She stops and waits, staring straight at GREG. *He can't take it for long and gets up, goes to the coffee area.*

GREG Wow, that's . . . you want milk?/ You sure?/ Lemme just . . .

CARLY No, Greg. Stop./ Stop it./ *STOP*! Sit.

He nods and returns to his seat. Quietly stirs his drink.

GREG Do you think we should . . . I mean, should we go home and discuss this, or . . . ?

CARLY Whose home? Yours or mine?

GREG Doesn't matter.

CARLY Yeah, it kinda does. I mean . . . at least *now* I know why we still have *two* homes.

GREG No, that's not . . . *no*. I promise.

CARLY Really? (*Beat.*) We did have the "move in together" talk a couple of times. . . so . . .

GREG Carly, absolutely not! (*Beat.*) I ran into Steph a few . . . not that long ago, and . . . we've just . . . we've . . . been . . .

CARLY She said she cornered you at Costco.

GREG Ok, yes. That's more like the truth . . .

CARLY I'd prefer the facts if you don't mind.

GREG . . . fine . . .

CARLY I guess this job is rubbing off on me . . . *that* and feeling like I'm suddenly back in the same fucking *nightmare* that I was in with Kent! (*Beat.*) Shit . . . / I can't even *believe* this!

GREG I'm sorry for not . . . / Carly . . .

CARLY I've gotta punch out so I'd appreciate it if you'd just jump in and say it, ok?/ *Please*, Greg? (*Beat.*)

GREG Carly, look . . . / I should've said something before, but I didn't know what to do—I did try to tell you once, I did!—but that's obviously why it's taken me so long to . . . for me to, to . . . *broach* this . . .

CARLY English, please.

GREG I'm struggling with what to do! I don't know how to handle this, so . . . I'm . . .

CARLY It's easy. Which one of us do you wanna be with?

GREG That's . . . we haven't had sex or anything, I promise. It hasn't been like that.

CARLY I know./ Steph said that, too.

GREG . . . oh./ She did?

CARLY Yeah, Greg, she told me everything. Girls are like that . . . honest. (*Beat.*) We fought for about, like . . . ten minutes . . . but the whole thing's just so fucking *absurd* that we . . . you know. We just got it out.

GREG Then . . . why didn't you say something? To me?/ No, I know that, I know, but . . . I'm just saying . . . if you *knew*, then . . .

CARLY Because it's not my place here, okay? I don't have to be the "guy" this time . . . / For the last three years I've had to do all the lifting and make the . . . be a mom *and* a dad to my daughter and I'm just not gonna do that in this situation. You are an adult, Greg . . . whether you like it or not. You have feelings—or at least I am giving you the benefit of the doubt—so you've got some idea how this should go by this point. So . . . go. Say something.

GREG . . . I'm . . . trying to . . .

CARLY However I feel about this . . . and I have a *shitload* of feelings right now . . . you and me are in a situation that we need to do something about. We gotta figure it out—I mean, *we're* not having sex, either, now and, so . . . I mean . . . what's going on here?

GREG I know. I *know* that . . . yes. It just didn't feel right . . . under the circumstances . . .

CARLY Is it me or her? (*Beat.*) Most people don't ever get a choice . . . or maybe, like, *one* time in their lives . . . but here you are. You got the two of us now and both of us are asking you to . . . whatever. Pick one.

GREG I don't wanna do *that*! I'm not . . . this is not how I wanted this to end up . . . !

CARLY Yeah, but it did! (*Beat.*) I'm not saying you lied . . . even though you kinda did—you *paused* or whatever—and I get that, I do . . . we all know each other so there's a history and, and . . . then with the baby stuff happening . . . it's a mess. (*Takes his hand.*) I understand, Greg . . . and I'm not yelling or mad at you, but you need to tell me what's going on. I am not gonna be run around on or, or become some, you know, one of those girls who goes chasing after the car of their boyfriend . . . I just won't fucking do that!! So tell me what's in your head./ Just say it . . .

GREG . . . Carly . . ./ God. This is . . . I like you *so* much, I really do . . . I know we haven't . . . I don't think either one of us has ever said "I love you" yet or anything, but . . .

CARLY . . . you don't "think" so?

GREG Ok, I know we haven't! (*Beat.*) Please tell me you didn't say it once and I missed it or something . . . I didn't, right?

CARLY No, you didn't. (*Beat.*) I haven't yet.

GREG . . . ok, good. I mean, not "good," but . . .

CARLY And I'm not gonna say it right now—I'm not going to make this *easy* for you, so you're stuck. Figure it out./ Just suck it up and tell the truth.

GREG I'm . . . Shit . . ./ (*Beat.*) If I was to say . . . if I *did* feel like Steph and I might have one more chance—I'm not saying that, either, I'm just *asking* you—what about the baby?

CARLY . . . / I'd take care of it, I guess.

GREG What?/ Great. (*Beat.*) Wait . . . what's that mean?

CARLY Greg. The hell do you think it means?

GREG You mean . . . I wouldn't want you to do it all by yourself . . . I'd be there for you, I hope you know that. I *totally* would.

CARLY . . . ok . . . thank you . . .

GREG And I've been going over and over this in my head because I think you're amazing . . . I really do, Carly, so . . . and I want . . . I'm feeling like . . ./ With what you've said . . .

CARLY Yeah?/ (*Beat.*) *What*?

GREG No, I'm not saying kids have to have two parents or, like, a father, even, because you've done an incredible job with being a . . . with Jennifer. (*Beat.*) But either way, I'd like to stay involved, whatever we do here. Either way./ Share custody, or . . .

CARLY No, wait . . . / That's not what I meant, Greg.

GREG . . . yeah, but I'm just saying . . .

CARLY You misunderstood me. I didn't mean "take care of it" as in raise the baby./ That's not what I'm saying.

GREG Oh./ But . . . so then . . . what're you . . . ?

CARLY I'm saying if we don't stay together then I'm going to "take care of it." (*Beat.*) Is that not clear enough for you?

GREG . . . you mean . . . ?

CARLY Yeah.

GREG But . . . no . . . we can't . . . no, no, no, no . . . !

CARLY Ummmm, yeah, Greg, I can. I can do that if I need to or whatever, *want* to, even, if I'm on my own. (*Beat.*) It's not a *we* thing. It's only a *we* thing if you're *with* me. Do you get that?

GREG Carly, wait, that's . . . I can't possibly be asked to . . . / No, hold on, seriously. This is a *huge* thing that . . . you know? *Wait.*

CARLY *What*?/ Obviously I *know*, Greg! Yes. But I also know that I can't do this again . . . be a single mom to another child and have to try and . . . I'm just not gonna face that again, I don't have to, it's not *1845* any more so I have options and that's just a fact. (*Beat.*) I am not blackmailing you on this . . . this is not a threat . . . it's just a fact about me and our, like, situation . . . (*Beat.*) Neither one of us asked for this, we just . . . we found each other at a time where it made sense but we were also in need, you know? *I* was. And maybe . . . look, it doesn't matter. I like you . . . I could even fall in love with you with just a little *nudge*, but . . . I also know that you and Steph have a *ton* of history so that's not . . . (*Tosses her hands up.*) Why am *I* the one doing all the talking here? I mean . . . Steph warned me about this! This is *so* "you," Greg . . . you let stuff happen to you, it happens and you just go with it but guess what? You are in the *thick* of it now, you're dead in the middle of this and you've gotta choose a direction to move . . . you do. You can't just *ride* it out . . . ok? (*Beat.*) Your turn now, so go. (*Beat.*) *Go.*

GREG *just stares at her. Trying to figure out what to say and how to deal with this. He weighs each word carefully:*

GREG Ok . . . listen . . . I'm just gonna say whatever comes into my . . . that'll be the best thing so I just . . . yeah. Here goes.

CARLY Wait. Just . . . (*Grabs his coffee and then gulps the rest of it down.*) I'm ready now.

GREG I think . . . / *Please*, Carly . . . this is hard enough! God! That's just cruel . . .

CARLY . . . did I mention that Jennifer is *really* happy being around you . . . ?/ I'm kidding.

GREG I'm in a real *spot* here, ok? Trying to sort out my life these days . . . and it's been a blast being with you, I love it. You're *so* beautiful and, and . . . *fun* . . .

GREG *is searching for a word and* CARLY *waits. Finally:*

CARLY But . . .

GREG *But*: I've been sending out resumes for, like, teaching jobs all over the place, in different *states* even, because that's my dream, to have a full-time position in English and to . . . so I don't know how that kind of thing sits with you . . . what with your mom here and, and . . . there's Kent to consider . . .

CARLY *rolls her eyes at this but* GREG *keeps talking.*

GREG No, we have to because like it or not, he is a factor here, Jennifer is *his* daughter . . . and then, you know . . . this whole "Steph" thing happens! We just—and now she's left Tim and I haven't even . . . I do love her . . . I mean I *say* that or did, anyway, to her, "I love you" but . . . have I *really* thought that through? I don't know! I felt like I did but then you tell me I'm gonna be a father . . . with *you* . . . and that makes me just . . . my heart gets all, like, *so* . . . . (*Gesturing*.) You know? *Full*.

CARLY . . . *and* . . .

GREG *And* I'm *trying* to explain! (*Beat*.) Look, I feel like I could love *you* . . . but it just seems bad to tell you right now, when I just said it a second ago . . . about Steph, I mean. But yeah . . . I think that's what I'm saying. That's my . . . you know . . . *that's* what I'd like to do, is find a way to be with you. A *path* that leads me back to *us* and to this thing that we started. I know that'll take some work but I'm up for that, I want to *do* it . . . to . . . *venture* off that way and forget the . . . you know . . . the past. *My* past with Steph, or . . . whatever . . . and be yours. (*Beat.*) So, yeah . . . (*Beat.*) *There*! I did it!

CARLY . . . did I . . . miss something?

GREG No! Didn't you *hear* what I just said?

GREG *looks at* CARLY, *waiting for some kind of response.*

CARLY I mean, yeah . . . but it was, like, the *Gettysburg Address*.

GREG Come on! Jesus . . . that was the *hardest* thing I ever had to say before! Please don't . . . like, make *fun* of me . . .

CARLY I'm not! I just . . . did you slip in there somewhere that you'd rather be with me?

GREG That's what I . . . yes! That's *exactly* what I was trying to say during the whole last part!

CARLY Ok. Good. But . . . / . . . I'm . . .

GREG What?/ Was that the wrong answer?

CARLY No, no, I just . . . but is it what you want? "You?" I mean, is it really, Greg?

GREG It's . . . I don't know! Yes!/ *Yes*. Under the circumstances.

CARLY Yeah?/ If it is, then great, but it had a little bit of a sound like something that you think you "should" do . . . like it's your *duty* or something./ And that's not what this is . . . I'm not the *Alamo*. No one's gonna *make* you do this, Greg.

GREG Carly, stop./ I *just* . . . did you not catch the part about me being able to fall in love with you? I wanted that to be, like, the real . . . *showstopper* . . .

CARLY It only stops the show if you mean it. Otherwise it's just . . . *juggling* . . .

GREG . . . I do, Carly! It's important to be . . . you know. Faithful. Here. To you, I mean.

CARLY "Faithful." I don't need a *dog*, Greg. I need a man./ I think you need some more time./ Yeah, you do . . . a little bit, anyway . . .

GREG No, I know!/ No . . . / Wait, *listen* to me!

CARLY *gathers her things.* GREG *gets up and goes to her. Tries to hold her but she's not having it right now.*

CARLY Greg, don't. Not right now.

GREG . . . I'm just trying to . . . I wanna hold you.

CARLY That's fine. Later. (*Beat.*) I'm tired and I need to go. I gotta think.

GREG *tries one more time to make contact but* CARLY *just gets further away.*

GREG . . . but . . .

CARLY I said "later," ok? (*Tries to smile.*) Call me after work or something.

GREG Ok. Do you wanna . . . or maybe dinner?

CARLY Maybe. (*Touches him on the cheek.*) Have a good day.

She tries to go but he puts his hands out and holds her—lightly but keeping her there in front of him.

GREG Wait . . . / Listen . . . you wouldn't really go to a doctor . . . I mean . . . not without talking to me first. Right? (*Beat.*) *Carly*?

CARLY What?/ . . . I guess we'll just have to see.

With that she walks out. GREG *is left standing in the break room. Alone. Unsure.*

The familiar buzzer blows. A few times.

The ball field.

GREG *sitting on a bench. Off by himself. He carries a book but he isn't reading. Instead,* GREG *stares into the distance. Thinking.*

After a moment KENT *arrives. Wearing sports gear. He has shorts on and one of those "touch football" belts around his waist. At least one flag is missing.*

He sits heavily on the opposite end of the bench. GREG *notices a bruise on his face. A band-aid over one eye.*

KENT . . . you should see the other guy.

GREG I bet! (*Pointing.*) Tell me you didn't get into it with one of your ten-year-olds . . .

KENT *No*! Dick! (*Laugh.*) Although there's some tough little fuckers out there, I gotta say . . . they get kinda rough. (*Touches his eye.*) *This* was something else.

GREG Huh. You need anything?

KENT Nah, you know . . . I got pretty thick skin.

GREG True. You do have an amazing ability to bounce back pretty fast . . .

KENT Yep. My *one* good quality!

Silence as they watch the youth football team practice. KENT *suddenly screams at some kids in the distance.*

KENT Awww, come on! (*Pointing.*) Get that guy!!

GREG . . . if you need to get back . . .

KENT No, I'm fine. Told one of the other guys to take over . . . we're just running plays.

GREG That's cool. (*Beat.*) Football was never my thing . . .

KENT No shit, buddy. Very little *reading* out there on the field.

GREG True! That's true . . .

GREG *is about to say more but stops himself. Silence.*

KENT So, thanks for coming. I know I called you outta the blue, so . . . thanks.

GREG No problem.

KENT 'ppreciate it. I just . . . I didn't know who else to talk to about all this . . . and . . .

GREG I'm happy to, man. Don't worry about it. What's up?

KENT Just stuff.

GREG Okay. (*Beat.*) You want me to *guess*, or . . . ?

KENT No, dude, obviously not—you probably *can* anyway, but whatever.

GREG Ummmm . . . the ever-popular "Crystal?"

KENT Yep. (*Beat.*) I got into a thing two nights ago and so . . . fuck . . . I dunno. I think I'm gonna lose my job.

GREG *What*?

KENT Uh-huh. (*Beat.*) It was that one asshole . . . the guy who originally hired Carly and gave her the security job?/ That guy.

GREG Right . . . / I know who you mean.

KENT That fucker was always up on her, with his little suit on and his . . . fucking . . . what's the thing right here? Tucked in his jacket pocket . . . ? (*Gestures.*) What is that thingie called?/ It's not a *handkerchief* . . . is it?

GREG Ummmm . . . / It's a pocket square, I think.

KENT Yeah, maybe that's it. Anyway, he was at the place, where I was with Crystal and a few of her friends, mostly these girls . . . and, I mean, I was over getting us some more drinks—Crystal likes those fucking *Mojitos*—and I come back and he's right there, up against her practically, just leaning in and smiling. Like, *rubbing* up on her . . . and so, shit, I tap him on the shoulder . . . you know? I'm not rude about it, I just . . . whatever . . . it's a tap.

GREG You sure?/ . . .

KENT Dude./ Fuck, come on! Whose side are you on here?

GREG No, I'm just saying . . . your "tap" can be a little bit aggressive sometimes . . . and yes it sounds like this guy's being a massive fuckhead, but . . . still . . .

KENT It's a tap. Ok? A "tap." (*He taps* GREG.) Like that.

GREG (*Reacting to it.*) Yeah, alright . . . but that's . . . it actually hurt, when you just did that./ Seriously.

KENT Fuck, fine!/ Everybody's a fucking *pussy*, is that what you're telling me?/ The whole goddamn world?

GREG No./ I'm not saying that. I'm saying I wasn't there so, you know, that is why I asked you "how" you did it.

KENT Not-very-hard. (*Beat.*) I've been working on my temper so, yeah, it wasn't bad . . .

GREG Fine.

KENT Ok, then. I *tapped* him—probably even a bit less than what I just did to you—and he turns and gives me a *look*, like, this "hey bro, I'm talking here . . . " and I'm, like, you know . . . "Fuck this."

KENT *touches his band-aid for a minute.* GREG *is silent.*

GREG What'd you do, Kent? (*Beat.*) *What*?

KENT What do you think I did? I smacked him. I was gonna let it go at that, I really was, but then he said some shit—and his forehead is sorta gashed by this time—and he starts in about *Carly* and *you* and, you know, a few other comments that just—and so I beat the living shit outta that guy. Like, bad. (*Beat.*) The cops came and everything. I'm pretty sure I'd stopped hitting him about that point . . . I must've stopped, 'cause that took a little while, for them to arrive . . . but I'm not sure, I was just so fucking . . . fueled up by that stage . . . and then they took him off to the hospital. (*Beat.*) I spent the night locked up—motherfucker's pressing charges over what's happened—I've gotta go in Monday and meet with the, you know . . . the fucking *owners* and shit.

GREG Jesus. That's . . .

KENT Yeah.

GREG He got in a few punches, though, I guess. (*Pointing.*) Or was that the cops?

KENT Actually, *that* I got from Crystal during the fight. She hit me on the head with her purse . . . some little metal part got me right here. A zipper, maybe, or—(*He yells toward the boys.*) Come on Brandon! Dig deep! (*Points at his eye.*) I didn't even feel it at the time but some guy, one of our delivery guys . . . he sent me a photo on his phone that he took of my whole face and, you know, shirt and everything was *totally* covered in blood. (*Gets out his phone and finds it.*) Here. Look. Huh?

GREG *considers this for a moment. Taking it all in.*

GREG Holy shit . . . I don't know what to say.

KENT I don't need you to say anything. I just wanted to tell somebody . . .

GREG . . . and so . . . did Crystal get all . . . ? I'm just asking because you said she hit you so that doesn't sound too good.

KENT Ha! No, not great . . . (*Beat.*) She moved her shit out last night. To her friend's.

GREG . . . no . . .

KENT Yep. She's gone. Left me this nasty note and called me a bunch of fucking . . . just some mean shit . . . she has this *terrible* fucking temper on her! *Un*-real some of the shit that came outta her . . . such a pretty face but, like, when she got mad you couldn't even *believe* it was the same person! Like one of those ladies with all the what-do-you-callems . . . you see in the movies . . . with, like, *snakes* in her hair? I mean, just, *totally* fucking psycho . . .

GREG *Medusa*?/ Sounds like it./ Wow.

KENT Is that who I mean?/ Then I guess so./ Yeah. It's just . . . you can never really tell with chicks.

GREG No, people are—not just women, but lots of folks, *guys*, too—they can have very surprising sides to their personalities.

KENT Yeah, but girls especially. Once you fuck 'em they get different. You know?/ Anyways, yeah . . . she's gone.

GREG Well, that's . . . / . . . sorry, man.

KENT Awwwwww, matter of time, really . . . that's how it always felt to me. With Crystal.

GREG Yeah?

KENT Uh-huh. Even from the beginning . . . she's not the kinda girl you can hold onto for long. (*Beat.*) I *was* the first guy to fuck her in the ass, though!/ I mean, *as* she was licking out one of her girlfriends. She told me she'd never done *that* before. Neither one of 'em had . . . which is cool.

GREG . . . *great.*/ You know what? That's too much info, Kent . . . *way* too much sharing for my taste.

KENT Doesn't matter. I'm just telling you.

GREG Terrific.

The guys watch the action for another minute. Suddenly:

KENT GO, YOU LITTLE BASTARD!! (*Points.*) Shit, I think he's . . . yeah, he's running in the wrong direction!! You stupid fucker! (*Signaling.*) BRANDON, WAIT! TURN AROUND!! (*Beat.*) YES, THAT'S IT! GO! GO!! JUST FOLLOW THE MAGIC LINES!!!

Apparently a touchdown is scored and the boys stand up and cheer. A quick high-five and some laughter. After a moment, they plop back down on another part of the bench.

KENT Fucking kids! I *love* working with these guys . . . they're *so* awesome.

GREG *nods and waits a beat, letting* KENT*'s thought hover in the air.*

GREG . . . so . . .

KENT Yeah. "So." (*Beat.*) They're gonna appoint me a lawyer and I guess we'll just roll with it . . . see what happens. I'm pretty clean./ I got a DUI and this thing from a few years ago . . . but I should be ok.

GREG Good./ Lemme know if you need anything—like a character witness or whatever. Do they do stuff like that anymore?

KENT I dunno. Probably just in your *books* . . . (*Grabbing up* GREG*'s novel*) John Steinbeck. *Sweet Thursday.* (*Tosses it back down.*) Fuck! Do you *ever* read anything good?

GREG Nah. Same old shit.

KENT Whatever makes you happy, I guess . . . (*Back to the kids on the field.*) CODY! Come *on*!!

GREG *turns his head at this. Thinking.* KENT *stands up to watch another play. Shakes his head and sits back down.*

GREG Hey. Do you think *you're* happy, Kent?

KENT . . .

GREG I'm just asking . . .

KENT Shit. "Happy" about what?

GREG Nothing. I was just wondering . . . after you said that.

KENT You really are, like . . . an odd fucker. You know that about yourself, right?

GREG For around here, maybe. Yeah.

KENT No, but seriously . . . I don't know!! Does *reading* make you "happy?" Like, honestly "happy?"/ *Really*?

GREG I think it does./ Yeah. (*Beat.*) Yes.

KENT Not me. Never even one time . . . I fucking hate books. *Despise* 'em . . . and I mean Dr. Seuss or fucking Hardy Boys, any of that shit. (*Thinking.*) I can't remember a time when the first thing I'd do is pick up a book. Not *ever*.

GREG That's too bad . . .

KENT I don't think so. It's like anything else that you either do or don't . . . you like or don't like . . . it's just a fact. You read, I don't. I play football, you don't. One isn't better than the other. Right?

GREG . . . awwwww . . . you're setting me up here.

KENT No, I'm *asking* you—do you think that's a better thing? Not "better" but, like, you became a *greater* person because of it?

GREG I dunno. I think that I enjoy it and it's also an escape, so there's that . . ./ And it's also a way of improving myself . . .

KENT Yeah, ok . . ./ . . . but has it made you some kind of *finer* man, though? Are you nicer with people or have you, maybe . . . would you say girls want to be around you more due to the fact that you read . . . has it really ever made a difference in your life?/ Yeah?

GREG I think so./ *Inside* myself, yes. It has.

KENT Huh. I don't see it, but hey . . .

GREG It's just an internal thing then, maybe.

KENT Maybe so. Just seems . . . *selfish* to me.

GREG *What*? How so?

KENT Listen . . . you're taking all that shit in and, yeah, maybe you'll teach it again or you could tell me the *theme* of some book but *think* of all the stuff you could've been doing otherwise . . . building churches or volunteering at some . . . nursing home . . . (*Beat*.) Sometimes you gotta just *do* something, you know? Not *talk* about it or . . . like . . . *think* it to death. Even if it's a fucking mistake—and I've made plenty of 'em, believe me—you just gotta go for it. You gotta . . . *man up* and . . . whatever. Make a stand.

GREG *nods, taking all this in while mounting a rebuttal.*

GREG . . . I'm not getting all defensive here, but it's weird to hear you telling me about "building churches" or, whatever . . . when you're . . . you know . . .

KENT What?/ No, go ahead, say it—because I'm not a college guy? Or been arrested?

GREG Nothing./ *No*, not that . . . but . . . anyway . . . have *you* ever built one? A church, Kent?

KENT No, not an *actual* church, but I've done a lot of community work with kids and that kinda thing. "Big Brothers" and shit . . .

my coaching thing here. Scouts./ Not in a "showy" way but just me helping out . . .

GREG . . . yeah . . . ok . . . / No, that's true . . .

KENT And that's all. (*Beat.*) You do what you want, man, it's just my observation . . . I just think reading is kinda useless.

GREG Huh. Well, really glad you called me down here today!/ You're such a feel-good guy!!

KENT Ha!/ Don't listen to me! I just . . . (*Beat.*) All I *mean* is . . . even if you *do* something *stupid* . . . at least you're still *doing* something.

GREG *takes all this in, carefully pondering* KENT*'s simple thesis.*

GREG True. (*Beat.*) Anyway . . . I might put it to use soon . . . I think I got a job for next term. A position in a *Montessori* program . . .

KENT I don't know what that is.

GREG It's education based on a . . . *constructivist* model.

KENT . . . I don't know what the fuck that is, either!/ You gonna be a *teacher* or not?

GREG Ha!/ Yeah . . . I'd be teaching. In an Arts program. English and Lit.

KENT . . . I suppose that's a cool way of saying "literature," right? "Lit."

GREG Sorry! Yes.

KENT You are so fucking queer now that you got your degree! Another week or two and I'll expect to hear you're on *Twitter* . . .

GREG Ha! No chance, man . . . I'm gonna have to draw the line somewhere!

KENT Good! Otherwise, I might really have to punch you if that was the case . . .

GREG Ha! You could try.

What follows is one of those things that builds. Not angry, but guys playing rough. Escalating with each blow. KENT *punches* GREG *on the arm.* GREG *does the same in return to* KENT. *This happens a dozen or so times, maybe more.*

GREG Alright, alright, I give! Fuck! Owww!

KENT Not bad for a fucking . . . cocksucker . . . (*Rubbing his arm.*) Shit! You hit me on my funny bone on that last one! Ahhh!

Both of them flex their arms and sit back down. Silence.

KENT . . . Carly going with you? Wherever you're going?

GREG It's in New York . . . if I go.

KENT *New York*! Fuck! Why would you *ever* go there?

GREG I dunno . . . it could be cool./ Shut up!

KENT Dude, people try to blow it up for a *reason*!/ I'm serious! AIDS started in that city. *All* kinds of shit . . . I don't want my kid growing up there!

GREG It's not *in* New York City. It's outside.

KENT Still.

GREG Yeah, well, that's where I just might be.

KENT Oh./ I hear "I" so what does that mean? You going *with* somebody or . . . just . . . ?

GREG . . . / Not sure.

KENT O-K. (*Beat.*) *Privileged* info or you just don't have an answer?

GREG The latter.

KENT *What*?

GREG I dunno yet.

KENT Yeah, well . . . tell Carly I'd get back with her if she ends up staying here.

GREG *Right.*

KENT I'm not kidding, man . . . in a heartbeat. Her *and* my kid. Absolutely.

GREG Ummmm . . . I don't know if we should get into that right now . . .

KENT Yeah, alright. *Fine*. I'd probably just fuck it up again anyways . . . (*To the kids on the field.*) That's right, guys! Keep it up!

KENT *turns his head away from* GREG. GREG *carefully watches his friend's behavior.*

GREG You ok?

KENT I'm fine.

GREG Yeah?/ Honestly?

KENT Yep./ Uh-huh.

GREG *Positive*?

KENT I'm good . . . I'm . . . / . . .

GREG What?/ *What*, Kent?

KENT *doesn't finish this thought—instead he stands up to watch another play happen. He sits back down and suddenly he starts to cry. Just like that. Tears.*

GREG *puts an arm around him but* KENT *never looks over at him again.*

GREG You sure you're alright?

KENT I dunno, man. I really don't know.

GREG *keeps his arm around his friend and* KENT *doesn't try to hold back now. He puts his head down and lets go. His shoulders heaving. Long, painful sobs.*

At work.

Break room, empty at the moment. Quiet. A buzzer suddenly shatters the silence. Once. Twice.

After a moment, STEPH *enters, followed by* CARLY. *It seems a little awkward between them but they try to smile and make small talk.*

STEPH . . . is this ok? I mean . . .

CARLY It's fine—it's usually pretty quiet up here until day shift comes on./I mean, unless fucking *Kent* shows up.

STEPH Ok./ Oh yeah . . . that'd be great.

CARLY Anyway, better than you sitting out there in the *lobby*./ Waiting for . . .

STEPH Thanks./ Right.

CARLY So, what? He told you to *meet* him here, or . . . ?/ That's . . . 'cause he called me to say he was coming here to see me . . .

STEPH Yeah./ Oh.

CARLY Why would he do that? (STEPH *shrugs.*) Not that you know, but . . . it just seems strange to me.

STEPH I didn't know if you'd be working . . . but I felt like I *had* to come. You know? He made it sound so . . . serious.

CARLY Plus, aren't you supposed to get there first?/ I mean, if you ask somebody to meet you . . . at a place . . . ? Isn't *that* the way it works?

STEPH Right?!/ Usually. (*Beat.*) Listen, I don't wanna re-hash any shit or . . . but I really am glad that we took the time to, you know, *talk* and stuff. The other day./ That made me feel better . . .

CARLY Me too./ Good.

STEPH I just felt like . . . whatever. Better.

CARLY I agree. (*Beat.*) *Greg* doesn't, but hey!

STEPH I know! That guy would rather run, like, a *thousand* miles than shout at a person or, or, or . . . disappoint someone.

CARLY Exactly!

STEPH He's always been that way./ He calls it "non-confrontational" or some shit . . .

CARLY Yup./ Convenient that they have a name for it . . . he probably thinks that makes it more "ok" if there's a name for it./ I mean, it drives me a little bit crazy, you know?

STEPH *No kidding.*/ Exactly! He thinks he's, like, Gandhi or some shit. Or the black one who got . . . (*Mimes a gunshot.*) Martin Luther King.

CARLY Yes!

They both nod in agreement and then check the clock.

STEPH I dunno . . . maybe women are just more . . . passionate or whatever.

CARLY We can *definitely* yell louder, I know that.

STEPH . . . anybody could yell louder than Greg . . .

CARLY . . . even Gandhi.

STEPH Or Helen Keller.

CARLY Who?/ You mean that one *blind* girl?

STEPH Nobody./ . . . yup.

The door opens. GREG *enters in a hurry and looks at them. Dropping his jacket and his bag on a nearby table.*

GREG . . . hey. Sorry I'm late.

Silence. GREG *re-groups and moves to each of them for a hug. Nothing big, but at least he seems sincere about it.*

GREG I was trying to beat you here, Steph, but traffic out on the highway gets . . . /So, forgive me.

STEPH Yeah./ Just so you know . . . I am not very cool with this. Having to come here.

GREG I understand./ Sorry, but . . .

STEPH This is . . . I don't like it./ It's weird.

CARLY I mean, I know you pick me up and stuff, but you don't *work* here anymore . . . / It's not like it's your private office.

GREG I *know*./ I wouldn't've asked to meet here if it wasn't important to me . . . okay?

CARLY Fine. I'm still on the clock, though, so—

GREG I'll keep it short. I promise . . .

STEPH Yeah, well, your promises don't seem to have that much weight anymore . . . so . . .

GREG Steph, please. Gimme a chance here.

STEPH I don't think we should all be meeting in a group like this, anyway. (*To* GREG.) *Why* are you doing this? Huh?

GREG . . . just because . . . I'm . . . / No, no, I just want us all to . . . be . . . on the *same* . . .

STEPH I think you're afraid./ You're afraid of getting yelled at again, by one of us . . . / Or if we did this in private . . . right?

GREG No, I'm not!/ No, Steph, I'm trying to . . .

STEPH I bet./ Uh-huh. *Sure.*

GREG That's not it. / No it isn't! (*Beat.*) Look, years ago I was here . . . in *this* room . . . it was, like, right after you came here and told me you were getting married, Steph, right after that . . . I decided to change my life and, you know, I have. Sort of. But . . . (*To* CARLY.) Kent actually challenged me on the subject a while ago—yeah, *Kent*—said he thought my reading was just a waste of time; he called it "selfish" and said instead I should be out *doing* something with my life and I thought about that. Was he right? Maybe. Maybe I have been selfish and not *done* enough . . . maybe I've just been . . . gliding along, going with the flow—even with the two of you—and that's not what you do in a relationship. You guys don't deserve that . . . either one of you. (*Beat.*) Anyway, look . . . the *big* news is this . . . I've taken a job in New York.

STEPH What?!

GREG Just *listen* . . . hear me out for a second.

Before GREG *can explain his ideas, however,* STEPH *reacts:*

STEPH . . . oh shit . . . are you gonna mess this up?! Huh?!/ Is *that* what you're getting ready to do?!/ (*To* CARLY.) And I'm sorry about the baby, but this is completely fucked! I mean, if you're . . . gonna . . . !/ OH SHIT!!

GREG No!/ Steph, please!/ I'm . . . / I am *trying* to help you understand where my head is at . . . / . . . and, and what I'm wrestling with here!

STEPH You said you "loved" me, Greg!/ That's *all* I wanna know right now . . . I don't care if it's here in front of Carly or not . . . do-you-love-me?

GREG I just . . . I *don't* know!

STEPH You asshole!!

GREG Please don't say that . . . / Just hear me out.

STEPH No, why?!/ *Why* the fuck should I?!

STEPH *gets up and goes to the door.* GREG *gets up to block her from leaving and* STEPH *lays into him. Kicking him and punching, too.* CARLY *jumps in and pulls her off of him.*

GREG Steph, don't!/ Stop that!/ Just lemme . . . !

STEPH You fucking, prick!/ You stupid fucker!/ I fucking hate you! Hate you!! HATE YOU!!

CARLY *pulls her friend aside and tries to hold her.* STEPH *shakes her off and stands in a corner.*

GREG *tries to move closer but knows to leave well enough alone.*

STEPH This is fucking bullshit, just your . . . usual . . . fucking . . . shit!!/ I gave up a *marriage* for this!!/ For YOU, Greg!!! For YOU!!!

GREG No, it's not!/ Steph!!!/ A MARRIAGE YOU DIDN'T WANT!!!

*That one stings—*STEPH *stops cold as* CARLY *tries to help:*

CARLY YOU GUYS! STOP!! (*Beat.*) Greg, just say what you wanna say and hurry up./ Go *on*.

GREG Fine./ OK. Can you guys *sit*? I mean . . .

STEPH I'm fine right here.

CARLY I have to go soon, so just say it.

GREG Whatever, alright. We can all . . . stand.

STEPH Yep. We're fine and we're standing. *Talk.*

GREG Okay . . . (*Beat.*) What I was *trying* to say was: I am not cool with this idea of me having to choose a life that either has you in it (*To* STEPH.) or you (*To* CARLY.) and someone is all mad or sad and that's not what any of us wants! So . . . I am drawing a line in the sand here—(*Looking at them.*)—I mean, obviously there's no "sand" but you know what I'm saying . . . this is it. I'm stopping the bullshit right *here*, right *now*. / I wanna begin again . . . start over and do it right.

CARLY Greg! / Get to the point.

GREG *checks to see how this has landed. The women seem to be listening but aren't revealing how they feel yet.*

GREG So like I said . . . I've got this job in New York . . .

STEPH . . . *shit* . . .

GREG Steph, just . . . (*Beat.*) I'm going to be teaching at this amazing school and my mind was going, like, a million miles an hour . . . You wanna know what I was thinking about, over the last few days . . . honestly? I was going to ask you both to come with me . . . *both*. Not in some—not *romantically*—but as "people," just as people I know, two people that I *cherish* and want to see great things happen to . . . (*Beat.*) I mean, "Why not?" Why couldn't we all just pack it up and get outta this town? Make new lives for ourselves and . . . ? And then I realized that's just me trying to have it all, both of you, and I have no right to do that . . . to feel that way. I'm barely able to take care of myself properly, so *why* should I have the right to ask you guys to do that. Huh? Well, obviously I don't, but I was actually able to get to that place, to *allow* myself to fantasize that we could all *waltz* outta here laughing and together, like some . . . some . . . (*Beat.*) But that's all that is, right? Just a *fantasy*.

STEPH Yeah. It sounds like something you read in *Penthouse*./ . . . *still* . . . it's gross.

GREG Steph . . . it's *not* sexual!/ Don't you see what I'm getting at here?! Come on!

STEPH No!

CARLY I think *I* do./ Yes. You *really* don't wanna hurt anybody's feelings here.

GREG Yeah? You do?/ . . . no, no, no . . . not just that, no . . .

CARLY You've gotten yourself into this place and now you don't wanna make us angry./ Or let anybody down. Right?

GREG *No*, that isn't . . . / I just wanna do what is right for *myself* and see if maybe that is at all attractive to you. *Either* of you.

CARLY Oh. I see. (*Beat.*) So, as long as you get *some*-body you don't care who it is . . . is that right?/ Is *that* your choice? *Any*-body?

GREG NO!/ No, I'm saying the opposite! I'm saying that I'm choosing "me!" I've realized that I need to be alone right now. I'm not ready to be with people, in *that* way, at least. I just . . . (*Beat.*) But: There are now also things that've been said . . . and/or *done* . . . and I'm here to do right by those, too, to be . . . there are *ways* to make this work! There *are*, if we just . . .

CARLY You don't have to worry about that.

GREG I know we can . . . what? (*Beat.*) *Why*?

CARLY Because you just don't.

GREG Yeah, but . . . wait . . . are you . . . ?/ What does that *mean*? That . . . you've . . . ?

CARLY *GREG. / STOP.* (*Beat.*) It's not an issue now, so scratch that off your list. It's done.

Silence. STEPH *touches* CARLY *and they look at each other.*

STEPH You alright?

CARLY I'm fine.

STEPH Yeah?

CARLY Uh-huh. (*Beat.*) Thanks, Steph.

GREG*'s on the outside of this but he's obviously worried.*

GREG . . . *Carly* . . .

CARLY You know what? You wanted an answer from us—or *each* of us, I guess—and my answer is NO. (*Beat.*) I could see what was coming and so I did what needed to be done. Even if we ended up together, you weren't ready to have a kid, Greg. You wanna go off and *find* yourself . . . but I'm looking for someone who wants *me* . . . not just my face, or my body, but me. Me and everything that goes with that. I don't think it's that much to ask for and I was willing to wait for you, Greg, I really was—and Jennifer loved being around you—we had a real chance there for a while . . . but hey. Your loss.

GREG Yes it is.

CARLY So for me it's not New York or teaching, any of that . . . I just need to be needed. And I don't think you're saying that to me—that you "need" me. *Me* alone. (*Beat.*) Right?

GREG Carly . . . it would be amazing to be around you some more . . . *and* Jennifer . . . I'd love that . . . and you're so great, I really do think we make good *friends* and I'm . . . we should . . . / You know?

CARLY Yeah. / I know.

Without another word, CARLY *gets up and gathers all of her gear. Goes to* GREG *and gives him a hug.*

Then, after a moment, CARLY *pulls away and slaps* GREG *hard across the cheek.*

CARLY . . . I'm not sure which one of those you deserve, but . . . you'll figure it out . . .

She touches STEPH *on the shoulder and goes to the door. Turns one last time. A little sadness in her voice:*

CARLY . . . shift change is pretty soon, so you guys should . . . (*To* STEPH.) He's all yours.

After she's gone, GREG *and* STEPH *look at each other.* STEPH *goes to the table and sits down.* GREG *follows her.*

GREG So. (*Beat.*) Did any of what I just said make sense? I mean . . .

STEPH Not really.

GREG . . . Steph . . .

STEPH *What*? (*Beat.*) I mean, yeah, I get it . . . I'm not stupid. Or *dumb.* But . . .

GREG But what?

STEPH When did all this happen? This . . . *New York* thing?

GREG I've been looking around for a while now . . ./ I mean . . . it's kinda been an ongoing thing . . .

STEPH Yeah . . . I guess you *have*!/ Shit. (*Beat.*) So you're gonna just . . . what? Move away now?

GREG . . . I don't have to go alone.

STEPH *thinks about this and nods. She finally speaks:*

STEPH Yeah, but you did the rest of it alone . . . I mean, you're not exactly asking my *opinion* here or, like, begging me to go *with* you. As a couple.

GREG Not yet, no . . .

STEPH *And* it's close to Rhode Island!/ Right?

GREG Ha!/ Yeah, no, you're right about that. It's fairly close to Rhode Island . . .

STEPH Fuck.

GREG But hey, lookit the bright side. At least it's not *Asia Minor* . . .

STEPH . . . you're such an asshole . . .

They sit for a moment. That damn buzzer goes off again. Long and loud.

STEPH How the *hell* did you ever stand that for so long?!

GREG Because it was a job . . . it was money . . . and at the time, we needed it.

STEPH That's true.

GREG Just like you . . . / Working at all those . . . cutting hair at the *mall*!

STEPH Yep./ So we could pay the rent and shit.

GREG You do what ya gotta do . . . when you're with somebody.

STEPH Right.

GREG Steph . . . *listen* . . .

STEPH I don't care what you think. I still feel like we're special. Like if we gave this another chance, that it might be . . .

GREG Maybe it would . . . but that's you . . .

STEPH No! *You* said it, too . . .

GREG For *you*. I said some of that stuff for you and because . . . (*Beat.*) *Yes*, I like us when we're at our best but right now . . . at this moment . . . standing in this fucking place that ate up so much of my life—that's why I asked you guys to meet me here! Because it's so symbolic of who I might've been . . . or ended up being—and I don't wanna be that guy . . . hell, I don't even wanna be who I am *now*! I wanna fix me and be happy. I want that, I do. And for you, too . . . and everybody. I want us all to be happy but I don't even know what that word means any more! "Happiness." I really don't . . . I mean, you can't touch it or, or taste it, so what the hell is it? I dunno! But I wanna get there, to "happy." To some "happy" place where I can just, you know, sit down for a few minutes . . . sit and do whatever it is that happy people do. That's what *I'm* looking for. (*Beat.*) I'm telling you the truth, Steph . . . I've gotta go do this! I can't keep reading books and, and listening to my old mix tapes and hoping for the best, figuring life will sort itself out if I just give it enough time. The time is *now*! I have gotta get out of here and try this on my own . . . and when I've succeeded at that then maybe I'll be . . . you know . . . ready for the next step, and the next one, and whatever else might happen after that. And then . . . if somehow you're still around . . . who knows?

STEPH Hmmmm. Don't count on it.

GREG I won't.

STEPH I mean, fuck . . . (*Beat.*) I guess . . . we can stay in touch if that's what you wanna do, but . . . / Fine.

GREG That'd be great./ I'd like that.

STEPH . . . or I could possibly come visit at some point, even . . . to check it out.

GREG That could work, too . . . (*Beat.*) I mean, you could always cut hair in New York . . .

STEPH Yeah. I could even open my *own* shop . . . or, you know. Something./ But I'm not gonna hold my breath.

GREG *Absolutely* you could./ I understand.

STEPH I feel like if there's a way to fuck this up, Greg, you will . . .

GREG *knows this is probably true and he smiles and looks away.* STEPH *watches him until he speaks:*

GREG *Thanks*. (*Beat.*) I really wouldn't hate it if you show up on my doorstep some day . . . just, like, you know . . . outta the blue.

STEPH As what? Your "friend?"/ You already have Carly for that . . . *apparently* . . .

GREG Maybe so. Maybe more./ *Steph*. Please . . . Anyway, I should be so lucky . . . I think *friends* with you would be great. I'd *love* to be your friend, Steph. I really would. (*He points to the door.*) You want me to walk you out . . . or . . . ?

STEPH Nah, that's ok. I'm just gonna . . . I need a minute alone. 'Kay?

GREG Sure.

GREG *slowly gets to his feet. Grabs his jacket and looks at* STEPH. *He touches her face. She responds.*

STEPH You're gonna miss this. (*Beat.*) I don't mean this place . . . or town or anything like that. (*Beat.*) You're gonna miss *me*.

GREG I know what you meant . . . and yes, you're right. No question.

They start to move together for a last kiss. Just as it starts the buzzer blasts again. STEPH *laughs and stops.*

STEPH Ok, fine! Fuck! I can take a *hint* . . .

They both smile at this and hug again. GREG *picks up his bag and moves toward the door. Opens it. Turns to* STEPH.

GREG Hey. (*Reaches into his bag and rummages around.*) I wanna give you something . . .

STEPH What is it?/ Better not be a goddamn book . . .

GREG Just . . . / Hold on . . .

GREG *pulls a rumpled volume out of his bag. Hands it over to* STEPH.

STEPH *turns it over a few times, studying the title. It is a* Fodor's Guide to New York City.

GREG It's not a book. It's a *guide*.

STEPH Thanks . . . (*Turning a page.*) If it says "To Carly" inside I'm gonna fucking smack you one . . .

GREG No! (*Pats his bag.*) I've got hers in here . . . (*Off her look.*) *Kidding*! It's mine.

STEPH *indicates she wants a look in his bag—*GREG *shakes his head then opens the bag and shows her. No more books inside.*

GREG It's got a *whole* section on "Hair Salons" in it, so . . . / You should really take a look sometime.

STEPH Good./ Yeah, maybe.

GREG I'm serious.

STEPH Ok . . . well, we'll see.

GREG God, you're a tough one!

STEPH Yep. I am. (*Smiles.*) But you like that . . . right? I mean, *secretly.*

GREG Yeah, I do. (*Smiles.*) And I don't even think it's a secret . . .

STEPH *looks over at* GREG. *Her eyes are moist but she is fighting it. Same thing for* GREG. *A long silence. She breaks the tension:*

STEPH . . . *so* . . . you feel any happier yet?

GREG Not yet. (*Smiles.*) But I'm working on it.

STEPH *simply nods.* GREG *almost speaks again but instead he nods in return, waves and exits.*

STEPH *sits for a moment. Takes several deep breaths and just manages to keep it together. She looks around.*

After a moment, STEPH *cracks open the book and begins to read. Turning the pages. Slowly she loses herself to the pleasure of the pictures and the places within.*

The lights pop off. Bam. Just like that.

ALSO BY NEIL LABUTE AND AVAILABLE FROM THE OVERLOOK PRESS

Neil LaBute burst onto the American theater scene in 1999 with the premiere of *bash* at NYC's Douglas Fairbanks Theater. These three provocative one-act plays, which examine the complexities of evil in everyday life, thrillingly exhibit LaBute's signature raw lyrical intensity. In *Medea Redux*, a woman tells of her complex and ultimately tragic relationship with her grade school English teacher; in *Iphigenia in Orem,* a Utah businessman confides in a stranger in a Las Vegas hotel room, confessing a most chilling crime; and in *A Gaggle of Saints*, a young Mormon couple separately recounts the violent events of an anniversary weekend in New York City.

"Mr. LaBute shows not only a merciless ear for contemporary speech but also a poet's sense of recurring, slyly graduated imagery . . . darkly engrossing."

—Ben Brantley, *The New York Times*

$14.95 978-1-58567-024-6

THE OVERLOOK PRESS • NEW YORK • WWW.OVERLOOKPRESS.COM